First published in paperback in Great Britain in 2011 by
HEADLINE PUBLISHING GROUP

1

Cataloguing in Publication Data is available from the British Library

ISBN 978 0 7553 7738 1

Typeset in ITC Stone Serif by
Palimpsest Book Production Limited, Falkirk, Stirlingshire

Printed and bound in Great Britain by
Clays Ltd St Ives plc

Headline's policy is to use papers that are natural, renewable and
recyclable products and made from wood grown in sustainable
forests. The logging and manufacturing processes are expected to
conform to the environmental regulations of the country of origin.

HEADLINE PUBLISHING GROUP
An Hachette UK Company
338 Euston Road
London NW1 3BH

www.headline.co.uk
www.hachette.co.uk

one

McKinley High parking lot, early Monday morning

The McKinley High School student parking lot was almost completely deserted. Even the faculty lot was only sparsely populated by a few cars belonging to overeager young teachers who had yet to reach the burnt-out phase of their careers. Snow had blanketed the town overnight, and it seemed as if the only sound in all of Lima, Ohio, was the scraping and whirring of the giant yellow snowplow as it pushed across the empty lot and deposited another load of snow on top of the already-dirty snowbanks. It was a brutally cold late February morning, and the lonely snowplow, driven by Janitor Bob, in his thick, dirt-brown coveralls and orange gloves that looked like giant oven mitts, was the only thing moving in the frigid air. A few chilly-looking birds sat on the telephone wires, probably regretting that they hadn't made the winter migration to a warmer climate.

'This is beyond pathetic,' Kurt Hummel said as he navigated his father's car into one of the newly cleared parking spots. 'No one else is even awake. And my leave-in conditioner barely had time to work overnight.'

Mercedes Jones yawned as she peered at her reflection in the passenger-side rearview mirror. She held her tiny green box of eye shadow and ran the miniature, doll-size brush across her eyelids, leaving a pale blue shine behind. She hadn't had time to put on any makeup before Kurt honked his horn in her driveway, and a no-makeup day just would not do. Especially not on a Monday. 'I don't get it. Why does Mr Schu really need to see us before school starts?'

'Maybe he discovered that torture is the best way to keep one's students from growing complacent.' Kurt slid the gearshift into park but didn't turn off the engine. He held his hands, in their sleek, black leather gloves, over the vents blowing warm air through the car. Although he enjoyed the cold Ohio weather, mainly because his winter wardrobe was fantabulous, his Alexander McQueen belted car coat was more aesthetic than functional.

'Look!' Mercedes pointed at the flagpole. An American flag normally flew at the top of it, when it wasn't being used by devious jocks to hoist up unfortunate underclassmen by their underpants, giving them the infamous 'patriotic wedgie'. But in honor of McKinley High's Multicultural Week, several foreign flags hung beneath the American one. 'Isn't that a Canadian flag? That seems like a strange culture to choose to celebrate – aren't they kind of just like us?'

'Yes, except they like socialism and hockey more than we do.' Kurt's eyes grew dreamy as he pictured burly guys with square jaws and broken noses hurling around on ice skates and pummeling one another into the clear plastic walls of the – what was it called? Hockey field? Court? No, rink. 'Hopefully the dining hall will not be celebrating the cuisine of our dear northern neighbors today.'

'What would it be? Canadian bacon?' Mercedes wrinkled her nose. One of the features of Multicultural Week was that the dining hall chose a different culture to highlight each day. She still remembered Polynesian Day freshman year, when dining services hauled in a pig on a spit with an orange in its mouth. Mercedes still hadn't recovered from that and couldn't even think about bacon – or pork or ham – without gagging.

'God help us.' Kurt made the sign of the cross, but, not being Catholic, he flubbed it. 'You know Mr Hausler will have a fit when he sees the American flag forced to share its noble post.' The balding civics teacher was a former Marine who vigilantly wandered up and down the aisles during the Pledge of Allegiance to make sure all the students in his first-period class recited – loudly – each and every word.

Mercedes's eyes scanned the grounds for other signs of life. Mr Schuester's beat-up car (the muffler actually touched the pavement) was sitting in the corner of the teachers' lot. There was already a faint dusting of snow on it, as if it had been there for a while. 'Seriously, are you worried that maybe there's something seriously wrong?'

Last night, all the members of Glee Club had received a mass text from Mr Schuester asking them to show up before school for an emergency meeting. It was an unprecedented move, and Kurt and Mercedes had immediately texted each other to discuss possible catastrophes that had happened to cause the extra-early morning meeting.

'You just used *seriously* twice in the same sentence.' Kurt's blue eyes scanned the message on his phone one more time for clues. Cryptic was not normally Mr Schu's style, although Kurt did like surprises. 'Seriously.'

'Correcting someone's grammar is a serious turnoff.' Mercedes stuck out her tongue at Kurt and tightened her hot-pink knit scarf around her neck. The windows of the car were starting to fog up, and she wiped clear a circle in her passenger-side window. She squinted as a blue car turned into the lot, its bald tires sliding across an icy patch. 'Finn's here,' she announced, recognizing Finn Hudson's oversized figure inside the car – his head almost touched the ceiling of the car. Mercedes opened the car door, letting in a blast of cold air. 'Let's see what he thinks.'

'Finn's not exactly known for his brilliant theories,' Kurt said affectionately as he grabbed his leather messenger bag and slung it over his shoulder. *Finn is known for other things*, Kurt thought. *Being the star quarterback, the star forward of the basketball team, homecoming king. His chiseled cheekbones. The way he can make tears spring to your eyes when he sings 'Faithfully'.*

As Kurt's leather ankle boots carefully stepped over the gray clumps of icy snow the plow had left behind, a familiar red minivan with a dented bumper pulled into a spot near Finn's. Mercedes waved a pink mitten at Tina Cohen-Chang, whose fingerless black gloves clutched the steering wheel. 'Hey, girl!' Mercedes cried when Tina stepped out of the minivan, a homemade knit cap with flaps tugged down over her ears.

Kurt tried to walk slowly so that they would pass Finn's car just as he got out, but Finn was playing with his radio and Kurt was forced to walk past it with Mercedes. A cold wind nipped through the air.

'You don't look like your bright-eyed and bushy-tailed self this morning,' Kurt said to Tina, glancing over his shoulder at the sound of Finn slamming his car door behind him. Perfect timing.

Tina blinked her eyes sleepily and shifted her faded-green canvas backpack, which she'd covered with patches of bands and inked doodles, higher up on her shoulder. Even though she looked exhausted, she'd still had time to put on bright pink eye shadow and thick navy eyeliner. 'I was up late working on the Chinese dragon costume.' Tina was a member of the small but enthusiastic Asian Student Union, and she had volunteered to rehabilitate the group's ancient dragon costume, recently dug out of storage in honor of Multicultural Week. The papier-mâché costume had warped since its last use, and Tina was pains-takingly reconstructing the parts that had torn off. She still had dried glue stuck to her fingers.

'What do you think this is all about?' Finn's deep voice asked from behind them. In his varsity letterman's jacket, he didn't exactly look like the kind of guy who would be caught dead talking to Glee kids, but he had changed a lot this year. He'd always thought he knew what he was going to do with his life – try to work hard and get an athletic scholarship to a big school, play football until his knees blew out, eventually get a decent job doing some-thing boring but well paying. It wasn't much, he knew, but he had a hard time visualizing a more exciting future. All he really knew was that he wanted to get out of Lima.

But things with Glee had kind of taken him by surprise and given him another option. He hadn't ever expected to join the group – thinking, like most people did, that it was a complete dorkfest – and then he'd actually ended up liking it. When the group won sectionals, his heart had wanted to burst. He thought back to the time last spring when he'd hit a walk-off home run in the division finals against Maryvale High, which had been the highlight of his athletic career, and it hadn't felt as good as when the judges handed the McKinley High Glee Club the giant gold trophy.

'We were debating, but we couldn't even decide if this meeting means good news or bad news.' Kurt glanced at Finn, whose handsome face was lined with worry. Despite the cold, Finn was the kind of hot-blooded jock type who didn't even own a pair of gloves, much less a scarf. Kurt had to admire that, even though he believed in taking advantage of every opportunity to accessorize.

'You think it could be *good* news?' Finn's face lit up as they all hurried up the freshly salted steps to the main entrance of the school. His cheeks were pink from the cold, and his just-showered hair was freezing into short hair icicles. 'I was afraid maybe he'd decided to be an accountant again.' There was a brief period last fall when Mr Schuester had considered leaving McKinley to work in an accounting firm so that he could better support his pregnant wife. He decided against it, which was fortunate because Glee Club really needed him. Also, his wife was only fake-pregnant.

The glass and metal doors clanked shut behind them. 'There's Artie.' Tina pointed ahead to Artie Abrams, who was wheeling down the hallway toward them from the cafeteria, where the school's only wheelchair-accessible ramp was located. She hoped it was nicely salted for him. They all paused and waited in the airy foyer for Artie to catch up. They wiped their wet feet on the industrial-size floor mat, which already seemed saturated with slush even though the day had only just begun.

'Did anyone catch *Pretty Woman* on cable last night?' Kurt asked, loosening his royal-blue cashmere scarf from around his neck. 'It's been on three times this month already, but I just can't look away.'

'You just like seeing Julia in her very fashionable street-walker attire,' Artie teased as he pulled up next to him. He was wearing his warmest winter coat, which his mom called his ski jacket – ironically, as he'd never skied in his life. He smiled faintly at Tina.

'What can I say? The black thigh-high patent leather boots get me every time,' Kurt said as he glanced at Finn, who looked slightly embarrassed. He was so easily scandalized.

Tina fell in step next to Artie. Things between the two of them had been . . . weird lately. Last fall, it had seemed like something was really happening. Artie was the only guy at McKinley High she could imagine herself with. He was sweet, and he had a wicked sense of humor. All the other boys seemed stupid and infantile in comparison. But things had sort of fizzled out before they really got started – maybe because she was shy and Artie was really insecure. Plus, Artie was really upset when he found out that Tina had faked a stutter. And now, so much time had gone by since they'd kind of gone to the homecoming dance together, Tina wondered if they'd ever be able to get things started again.

'It's *got* to be bad news,' Mercedes said, taking her baby blue earmuffs off her head and stuffing them into her pocket. Her tan Uggs squeaked against the clean floor, the noise echoing through the otherwise quiet hallways. 'Like, Mr Schu's had another change of heart and is leaving us to join the Peace Corps in Africa or something.'

'That wouldn't happen.' Artie's thick black glasses had fogged up when he entered the building – yet another disadvantage of wearing glasses. He'd considered contact lenses, but they didn't have the same gravitas. He removed his glasses and wiped them on his plaid scarf. 'Mr Schu would never leave us like that. Besides, he doesn't seem like the hands-on type. I can't really see him building a school.'

'Maybe our budget got cut again, and we're going to have to share the choir room with the wrestling team,' Kurt offered, raising his eyebrows. 'Maybe they could teach us some moves.'

'What if someone's leaving the club? Or dying of some weird kind of cancer that takes out your vocal cords?' Finn asked suddenly. He glanced over his shoulder at the sound of the doors opening and saw Matt Rutherford and

Mike Chang, football players who had also joined Glee Club last fall. They were usually the last to arrive.

Finn didn't want to say anything, because he felt like he was always bringing her up, but wasn't it weird that Rachel wasn't here yet? Even though they weren't dating or anything – at least, not anymore – he still had this kind of Rachel radar. A room, or a hallway, just felt different when she wasn't in it, maybe because she had such a big – and loud – presence. It was like he couldn't get her out of his head, even when he wanted to.

'Where's Rachel?' Tina asked as they turned the corner to the choir room, as if she had read Finn's mind. Rachel Berry liked to be the first one at any practice, meeting, or event, and it was weird that she wasn't standing outside the choir room, waiting impatiently for everyone else to arrive and chastising them for being one minute late.

There was silence except for the squeaks of their wet shoes against the linoleum floor as they approached the choir-room door, collectively pondering what it would mean if Rachel was gone. Finn immediately wondered if she'd done what she'd threatened to do a few months ago – transfer out of McKinley into a performing arts school where she could get the training she needed to become a star.

But . . . she would have told him, wouldn't she? He felt a lump in his throat. 'Maybe it's Rachel who has the weird kind of cancer. Maybe she *is* dying . . .'

Just as Kurt started to picture himself wearing his black fedora to Rachel's funeral and singing Elton John's 'Candle in the Wind', Mercedes interrupted his fantasy. 'I'm not sure cancer is strong enough to kill Rachel.'

Just then, everyone heard a noise come through the walls of the choir room. 'I think someone's in there,' Kurt whispered, feeling like he was in a Scooby-Doo cartoon. Finn, of course, would be Fred, the manly alpha male with the broad shoulders and the devastating chin.

Mercedes rolled her eyes. *Kurt can be such a drama queen.* 'If it's an axe murderer, I guess I'll be the first one to go.' She grabbed the door and pushed it open as everyone behind her peered inside.

Rachel, looking anything but dead in a baby blue plaid skirt and white mohair turtleneck sweater with a giant strawberry knitted into the front, had a look of incredible concentration on her face as she sang out a line from *Cabaret*. At home each morning, she drank her protein shake for breakfast and put in thirty minutes on her elliptical trainer, getting herself physically ready for the day. But her early morning practices in the choir room helped her get spiritually ready for it. (And there was the matter of her neighbor's threatened lawsuit if she continued to sing at 6:30 every morning.) She loved singing Liza Minnelli tunes in the morning – they prepared her to face the day, putting her in exactly the right mood to confront the haters and naysayers and those who, despite her success in Glee, insisted on continually throwing slushies in her face. Early morning practices were an integral part of her routine, and without them, she'd be lost.

It wasn't until she finished the verse that she felt something was wrong. She whirled around. Standing in the doorway, her fellow Glee Club members were crowded like groupies, gawking at her.

'What . . .' she started, glancing at the clock on the wall. 'What are you *doing* here? This is my private practice time.'

Mercedes's jaw dropped. 'You come to school this early every Monday just to get in some more practice time?' She threw her backpack down on a chair and unzipped her puffy coat. 'You're crazier than I thought.'

Rachel stared at the backpack, as if its presence was personally threatening her space. 'No, I come here every *morning* to practice.' She crossed her arms over her chest, feeling like she was under siege. The half hour before everyone else got to school was her sacred time. 'What are you all doing here?' She tried not to let her eyes land on Finn any longer than absolutely necessary. She was still trying to convince herself that she was over him.

'Didn't you get Mr Schuester's text last night?' Artie asked, rolling toward the first row of seats. His wheels left a faint trail of slush behind them.

'Text? No.' Rachel eyed her phone, which played 'I Feel

Pretty' from *West Side Story* every time it rang and pinged each time she got a text. 'I shut it off last night when I went to bed early, something I advise all of you to start doing as it helps the vocal cords repair themselves over-night.' She held her head high.

'Then why didn't you hear it when you turned on your phone this morning?' Mercedes sat down in a plastic chair and stared straight at Rachel. This girl had an ego the size of China and an excuse for everything. Mercedes just liked to give her grief.

Rachel met Mercedes's eyes. 'I guess I couldn't hear it ping over my incredible talent.'

Mercedes jumped to her feet. 'Oh, I'd like to take your incredible talent and see what it looks like when . . .' Before Mercedes could finish her threat, however, the door to the choir room flew open again. Mr Schuester entered, carrying a huge pink pastry box under one arm and a giant plastic jug of orange juice in the other hand. The sweet, fragrant smell of freshly baked pastries swirled through the air, and Mercedes immediately sat down. Her stomach rumbled, reminding her that she hadn't had time for her bowl of cereal before Kurt's car honked in the driveway.

'Hey, gang!' Mr Schuester's handsome face beamed at them. His curly brown hair, still wet when he left the house, had frozen earlier in the cold. 'I'm sorry to freak you all out by calling an early morning meeting, but I wanted to get the chance to talk to all of you and I couldn't wait until practice after school.'

'So what's the big news?' Kurt asked, eyeing the box. Something smelled delicious, and he wanted to know if it was something that was worth the extra calories. 'We've been frantic with anticipation.'

'Well . . .' Mr Schuester scanned the room. Mike and Matt stumbled through the doorway, looking barely awake. But there were no signs of Noah 'Puck' Puckerman, Quinn Fabray, or the two Cheerios – Santana Lopez and Brittany Pierce. 'I really wanted to tell everyone as a group, and it doesn't look like you're all here.'

'What?' Rachel, who had sat down when Mr Schuester entered, jumped to her patent-leather feet. She was always on the lookout for unfairness, and this was extremely unfair. 'But Puck and the Cheerios are always late. It's not fair to punish us for their faults.'

Mr Schuester's eyes glazed over slightly, as they often did when Rachel opened her mouth to express her opinion on something, which she did at least a hundred times an hour. 'Let's just wait and see if they show up.'

Finn, who was dying to tear into that pink pastry box, couldn't stand waiting anymore. He hoped there were jelly donuts in there. The kind that were covered in gritty sugar. 'Uh, Mr Schu? I talked to Quinn last night, and I, uh, don't think she's going to make it this morning.' Even though he and Quinn were not dating anymore, he still

14

cared about her. Maybe he shouldn't – especially after the way she had lied and told him that he was the father of her unborn baby. The real father was none other than Finn's best friend, notorious womanizer Puck. This fact alone should have been enough to keep him from ever even *thinking* about casting a sympathetic glance toward her pretty face again. But Finn was a big softie. As much as he hated what Quinn had done, he worried about her. Finn often pictured Puck with a baby on his knee, trying to feed it a spoonful of hot sauce or something. Poor kid. That was why Finn allowed Quinn to call him sometimes and talk about her day. What she'd said about the early morning meeting was, 'I might consider coming, if it wasn't for the fact that I have a standing appointment to puke my guts out at that exact time every morning.' But Finn didn't want to repeat that in front of everyone.

'Great.' Mr Schuester threw his hands in the air. 'Well, I'm sorry to drag you all here so early, but it looks like you're going to have to wait a little longer to hear my news.' Amid groans and frustrated glares, Mr Schuester held up the pink pastry box in self-defense and set it on the piano. 'But I did bring you some treats – take them as a peace offering. And how about we meet here again at the beginning of lunch period? I'll be sure to find the kids who are missing and let them know.'

Finn was the first to crack open the box. Two dozen buttery fresh croissants were sitting atop the box's white waxed-paper lining. Finn bit into one, and it nearly melted in his mouth. Even better than a jelly donut. 'Awesome. Thanks, Mr Schu.'

Everyone dove in. 'Enjoy, everyone. And remember – it's a clue.' He winked at them all but wouldn't say any more.

Rachel reluctantly poured herself a cup of orange juice. If her morning practice was going to be interrupted, it might as well be for a *reason*. Celine Dion didn't get to where she was today by canceling practice for some orange juice and croissants. Her day was already going downhill, and it wasn't even first period.

two

Hallway, between classes, Monday morning

The hallways of McKinley High were a dangerous place for those not blessed with an advantageous position in the social hierarchy of high school. Inside the classrooms, even the worst teachers managed to exert some sort of control over their more unruly students, and in the cafeteria, teachers alternated lunch monitor duties. The hallways between classes, however, were largely lawless stretches of real estate crammed with hormonal teenagers who were eager to expel some energy. Unfortunately, those who ranked lower in the high school caste system were often on the receiving end of unwelcome attention, which included anything – being tripped, pushed into lockers, or 'accidentally' jostled so that their books fell to the floor. The worst form of hallway torture was a slushie in the face.

Tina Cohen-Chang had an artsy, Goth style of dressing that made her stand out from all the kids in jeans and sweaters, so she was grateful every time she made it to her locker unslushied. Today she was wearing a knee-length yellow-and-black plaid skirt held together at the side with giant safety pins, a Blondie T-shirt, and a thick black cardigan with holes in the elbows.

'Bake sale,' she said to Artie, who, being wheelchair-bound, was also often the recipient of unwelcome hallway attention. Tina glanced at her history notebook, where she kept her locker combination written in blue ink, and spun the lock. She had a terrible time remembering it, especially on Monday mornings. 'It *has* to be another bake sale. Why else would Mr Schuester bring us croissants and tell us it's a clue?'

'I think croissants are really hard to bake, unless you use that Pillsbury kind that comes in a tube.' Artie reached around to his backpack, which he'd hung on the back of his chair. He'd just thought of a great line for a song he was working on, and he needed to write it down in his notebook before he forgot it. Someone behind him bumped into his chair – accidentally – and sent Artie skidding forward into someone's locker. 'And I don't think they're very high quality.'

Tina flung open her locker. 'I don't think I'm emotionally prepared for another bake sale.' On the inside of her locker door was a photo of Joan Jett, ticket stubs from the White Stripes concert she and Artie had gone to in Columbus last fall, and her favorite Georgia O'Keeffe quote, written in her careful calligraphy on a torn-out notebook page: *I've been absolutely terrified every moment of my life – and I've never let it keep me from doing a single thing I wanted to do.* Beneath those items was a photograph of Glee Club at sectionals, everyone beaming as Rachel and Mercedes held the heavy gold trophy in the air. Tina, despite the confidence singing gave her, was still nail-bitingly shy, and the thought of sitting behind a long table in the cafeteria and asking passing students if they wanted to buy a one-dollar cupcake made her want to cry.

'The last one was pretty brutal.' Artie thought back to last fall, when the Glee Club members had sat with their sad-looking cupcakes while students pretended not to see them as they walked by. He'd felt like one of those department store sales clerks who try to get uninterested shoppers to try a new cologne.

'You guys need to expand your thinking. It's not another silly bake sale.' A chipper Rachel appeared with Mercedes at her side, clutching a stack of books to her chest. Everyone in Glee Club knew they needed Rachel to be great – she had an amazing voice, and she knew so much more about performing than any of them did – but she was one of those people who had a habit of driving everyone around her crazy. Maybe it was her unfortunate habit of pointing out her strengths while simultaneously pointing out other people's weaknesses.

'I'm guessing you're going to go ahead and tell us what you think it's about, Ms Expanded Thinking.' Mercedes peeked into Tina's locker mirror and spread some straw-berry-vanilla lip gloss on her chapped lips. She was already annoyed with Rachel, who had asked earlier if Mercedes's giant gold star earrings were an homage to her. Rachel seemed to think the gold star was her own personal symbol.

'It's clear that Mr Schuester is simply honoring my repeated requests—' Rachel started to say before a passing senior in a basketball jersey thumped his fist down and knocked all of Rachel's books to the floor.

'More like *demands*,' Mercedes broke in, glancing at her phone as it emitted a *cheep* sound. Kurt had just texted: *maybe he wants us to incorporate some Cirque du Soleil moves*.

Rachel, ignoring Mercedes, bent down to collect her things. Tina stooped over to help. *Boys at McKinley High are so rude*, Tina thought. 'It's clear that he's just ready to honor my repeated requests to let us sing a selection from the seminal musical *Les Misérables*,' Rachel said.

Tina and Artie exchanged glances. Mercedes snorted,

thinking, *Rachel is sort of like one of those horse-size multi-vitamins – hard to take on an empty stomach.* 'I think it's a bake sale,' Tina said, slamming her locker closed.

Rachel sighed heavily and continued down the hall toward class. It was amazing that she accomplished anything with all the negativity surrounding her. But she wasn't going to let anyone's Debbie-downer attitude dampen her spirits, not when she had just won a triumph over Mr Schuester, who, for some odd reason, seemed like he was always trying to ruin her career. He was probably just bitter that he'd never made it on Broadway and was instead teaching Spanish and coaching Glee Club in the sleepy little town he'd grown up in. Maybe he'd finally realized that keeping her happy was the only way to ensure Glee Club's success and had at last accepted one of the approximately 185 suggestions she'd offered him this semester. It was about time.

For the past few months, it seemed like no one in Glee Club listened to her. Ever. It was frustrating, as she was the only one who had been performing since infancy, and they all had a lot to learn from her.

As she rounded a corner and was nearly plowed into by a couple of boys chasing each other with lacrosse sticks, Rachel caught a glimpse of the familiar red-and-white Cheerios uniforms at the end of the hallway. In the winter, Coach Sylvester's championship cheerleading squad cheered for McKinley High's basketball team. They slightly altered their uniforms by wearing white turtlenecks under the sleeveless tops that read WMHS and white leggings under the short pleated skirts that made boys salivate. She could never figure out why they wore them every day, but Rachel had a hunch that Coach Sylvester demanded it as a way to reinforce the status quo and remind the rest of the student body that the Cheerios were *important*, as if they could ever forget.

Rachel normally was not overly interested in the Cheerios, but these two happened to be Santana and Brittany – the girls who had skipped that morning's emergency meeting. They were leaning against their open lockers, looking lithe and beautiful and without a care in the world.

Rachel's eyes narrowed. *How did the two of them manage to have lockers right next to each other, anyway?* Coach Sylvester had all kinds of inappropriate pull. Not that Rachel objected to their being in Glee Club – without them, Glee wouldn't have the twelve members necessary to qualify for competition in the state, and the presence of members of the highest social stratum slightly raised Glee's status out of the sub-basement.

But it didn't mean they could treat Glee like it was nothing important. They'd completely ignored Mr Schuester's text, simply because they didn't really care about Glee. Or at least that's how they acted. One of them would often skip practice or show up egregiously late, sipping a Starbucks Frappuccino. And Santana once answered a text in the middle of a solo – that Santana was singing!

Rachel stepped around a couple of AV kids rolling a giant television monitor on a cart down the hallway and tried to inconspicuously get closer to the Cheerios. She feigned interest in the display case full of incompetent freshman watercolors and strained her ears.

If she'd expected them to be equally concerned about Mr Schuester's motives for calling his emergency meeting as the rest of Glee Club was, she would have been disappointed. 'It's called Mezzo, or something,' Santana was saying. She had a way of talking that made her sound bored even when she was excited. Maybe it was because she was always chewing gum. 'And it's the hottest new boutique at the mall since Express closed.'

'I heard that the designers are European, or maybe Italian.' Brittany examined herself in the magnetic mirror on the inside of her locker, smacking her lips to even out her shiny pink lip gloss.

Quinn Fabray, former head Cheerio, strutted up to join them. Even while pregnant, Quinn still managed to look gorgeous, with her angelic blond locks, heart-shaped lips, and gilded halolike headband. Rachel had heard about the 'pregnant glow' women supposedly got when they were expecting, but this was ridiculous. Wasn't her situation a popularity deal-breaker? Maybe in Quinn's case it wasn't, although she clearly hadn't come to school with Santana and Brittany that morning – a notable change in ritual for the three of them. Quinn desperately dove right into their mundane conversation. 'Shopping? I'm always up for a little retail pick-me-up. School is about four hours too long,' she said as she slung her backpack over her shoulders. 'Let's go after school and find some new outfits for the Basketball-Cheerios mixer this weekend. I don't have anything to wear.' That, of course, wasn't true. Quinn had a walk-in closet full of amazing clothing, thanks to Mrs Fabray's former need to have 'mother-daughter' bonding time, which mainly consisted of trips to the mall. But Quinn had to face facts. Her growing stomach had made most of her expensive jeans and dresses way too tight or altogether unwearable. And even though she should probably be saving her money for the baby, looking good was still a matter of pride for Quinn. So was attending the mixer like a normal teenager.

Rachel shifted closer. In her plaid skirt and sweater with puff sleeves, she usually would have felt like a five year old when standing next to Quinn and the Cheerios, but she was too annoyed at what she was hearing to feel self-conscious. Were they really talking about skipping after-school Glee rehearsal to go shopping? The group needed them, as much as Rachel hated to admit it, and they were about to let everyone down. Again. It was completely unfair.

'That's not good enough.' Santana shook her head, her long black ponytail swishing against the back of her uniform. 'We have to go ASAP. I saw on Facebook that all the really great stuff is flying off the racks.'

'Wait, lunch is when I walk my imaginary poodle around the cafeteria,' Brittany said. She hugged a folder with a picture of a kitten chewing on a ball of yarn. 'He'll be mad if I forget.'

'We could get those delicious low-fat berry smoothies at the food court, too,' Quinn added, giving a shy smile as a couple of jocks brushed past the girls, gently bumping them with their shoulders. Quinn never had her books shoved to the floor, Rachel was pretty certain. And she had to admit, it was amazing how effortlessly Quinn could turn on the charm. If only Quinn had talent equal to her looks, Glee Club would be much better off. She had a face that was born to be in a head shot. 'That's way better than the artery-clogging offerings found in the cafeteria, and I really can't stand to ralph again today.'

'Ew, Quinn. Anyway, I think it's Chinese food today, for Multicultural Week.' Santana wrinkled her pert little nose. 'I don't know how Chinese people stay so skinny. That stuff is loaded with carbs.'

Rachel took a deep breath and stepped forward. She tapped Quinn on the shoulder and got a face full of spinning blond ponytail when Quinn turned around. 'Yes?' she asked coolly, eyeing Rachel from head to toe. She preferred not to be seen speaking to Glee Club kids in public, especially now that she was unsure of her position on the social ladder – and Rachel knew that.

Rachel smiled sweetly and ignored the bitchiness in Quinn's voice. She would most likely have to deal with unfriendly critics once she became a Broadway star, and the Cheerios' meanness was good as preparation. 'I couldn't help but overhear . . .'

'Yeah, because you were totally *eavesdropping*.' Santana crossed her arms over her chest. 'I saw you lurking over there like some kind of stalking stalker.'

'Regardless.' Rachel cleared her throat and fingered the collar of her sweater. 'I just wanted to tell you that there's no way I'm going to let the three of you bail on Glee Club again today. Mr Schuester has a big announcement to make, and he needs us all to be there at lunch, as I'm sure he told you.'

Quinn almost choked on her laughter. Four months ago, she never would have imagined that Rachel would ever have the nerve to speak to her. Rachel was just a friendless loser who sat in the front row of class and almost peed herself with excitement every time she raised her hand. But now she was the star of McKinley High's Glee Club, and that gave her delusions of grandeur. She really needed someone to bring her down a notch. Or at least to be publicly humiliated, just as Quinn was when Rachel had revealed her big paternity secret to Finn. That privileged information totally wasn't Rachel's to tell anybody, let alone the guy Quinn was trying to claim as her baby-daddy. Quinn had actually felt relieved after the whole ordeal was over, but she wasn't going to let Rachel get off that easily. 'Oh, really? And what are you planning to do to stop us?'

Rachel smirked back at her, dropping her fake smile. 'How about I warn Principal Figgins about your constant ditching? I'm sure he'd be happy to keep a close eye on you for the rest of the semester to make sure you don't skip class again.' Rachel never minded being a tattletale. If people followed the rules in the first place, it would never be necessary. She made it a habit of visiting Principal Figgins's office once a week, whether she needed to or not.

The three girls' mouths fell open almost simultaneously. Quinn clenched her hands into little fists. Even though Brittany and Santana were Cheerios – and even though all the teachers, even Principal Figgins, believed Quinn was a perfect angel, pregnant or not – it didn't seem smart to call attention to the fact that they'd missed a lot of school lately. And she had no doubt that Rachel would very cheerfully skip right into the principal's office and throw them under the bus. 'You wouldn't dare,' Quinn finally managed to say.

'Try me,' Rachel said, feeling her confidence brim up. 'I know *you* don't, but *some* of us take Glee seriously.' She cleared her throat. 'So, maybe if you three decided to take it *more* seriously, I wouldn't need to say anything to anyone about your terrible class attendance.'

Santana shook her head. 'No way.' Rachel reminded Santana of her annoying little cousin who was always running to adults to tattle whenever the older kids were ignoring her. 'That doesn't sound like a great deal.'

'Santana's right.' Quinn's hazel eyes narrowed. Someone had once told her that she appeared to shoot daggers with her eyes, and she loved the way she could make a freshman girl quake by just giving her the right stare. 'We're going to need something from you in return. If you want us to show up at lunch and at practice today, *and* in the future, you're going to have to help cover for us when we do decide we need to leave campus.'

'What?' Rachel frowned. *Who did they think they are?* 'Why would I do that?'

'Because we could just quit Glee altogether, and then you wouldn't have enough people to compete at regionals.' Quinn hugged her biology textbook to her chest. 'And I have a feeling you don't want that.'

From the looks on the three girls' faces, Rachel could tell they weren't going to budge. Quinn was used to getting what she wanted, after all, and she knew she had the upper hand against Rachel. 'Okay, fine,' Rachel agreed reluctantly.

'Also,' Quinn spoke up, trying to think quickly, not

wanting to let Rachel get away with anything, 'there's something else.' It was ridiculous if Rachel thought she could just stroll right up and start making all kinds of unreasonable demands. Quinn did not take orders from a dweeby Glee girl with zero fashion sense and a nose too big for her face, and she knew that Rachel had two weaknesses, outside of her physical appearance – her devotion to Glee Club and her obsessive love for Finn. Finn was completely out of her league but somehow had been duped into a short-lived rebound fling with Rachel, which she definitely had not gotten over. 'You're not allowed to talk to Finn for two weeks.'

Rachel's eyes bugged out. Santana and Brittany giggled wickedly. They found it completely bizarre that Finn had ever been interested in Rachel, however briefly. Quinn, though, could understand it. Rachel was annoying, but she was talented and innocent and sincere, and those were all things Finn admired. Plus, Rachel was passionate and dedicated to her goals, traits that Finn was always striving for himself. So much so that he didn't pay attention to the fact that Rachel looked as if her grandmother dressed her every morning. In the dark.

'Wait, what does Finn have to do with anything?' Rachel asked. She knew Quinn was furious that Rachel had dated Finn after Quinn broke up with him, but she didn't realize she was still bitter about it. Maybe Quinn still held a grudge against Rachel for telling Finn he wasn't the father, which, admittedly, Rachel had done to break them up so *hers* could be the loving arms he fell into. But it wasn't even as if Finn and Rachel were together anymore – Finn had made it clear that he wasn't strong enough to deal with a high-maintenance, high-minded girl like Rachel.

Besides, Rachel had new romantic prospects on the horizon. She had recently run into Jesse St James, the star of the Glee kids' biggest rival club, Vocal Adrenaline, at the local music store. Jesse had let Rachel know that he had more on his agenda than making sweet music together. So there.

Quinn shrugged, barely able to keep the triumphant smile off her face. So what if she and Finn had broken up? It didn't mean she liked the idea of him moving on from her yet, especially not with a girl like Rachel. Quinn would prefer Finn to have tortured dreams about her for years to come, which was why she insisted that they still stay friends. Also, he listened to her complain about things, which was a valuable quality in a boy. She didn't know if she wanted to get back together with Finn – but she also didn't want him to be with anyone else. 'Maybe he doesn't have anything to do with it. But if you want us at Glee Club rehearsals, you're going to need to do it.' Quinn felt a teensy bit bad about manipulating Rachel, who had a pained look on her face, but she had to at least *try* to maintain her reputation as a girl who didn't back down.

Rachel bit her lip. She could feel the eyes of the three girls staring her down, and a thin line of sweat had formed between her shoulder blades. Now she knew why people didn't mess with Quinn or the Cheerios. They hit you where it hurt. But she wasn't about to let Quinn know how much Finn meant to her – even though she undoubtedly already knew. Quinn's tiny ears were faintly pointed at the top, and she seemed to have the uncanny ability to sense other people's weaknesses. And Finn was Rachel's weakness – her only one, she liked to think.

But, regardless, Rachel's career was more important than her need to flirt with Finn. He'd had plenty of times to ask her out again, if he was ever going to, so it wasn't like Rachel was giving up on a sure thing, by any means. She'd had her moment with him, and now it was over. Maybe it was time she accepted that.

And it was just two weeks, right? Mr Schuester's news had to be worth it. Glee needed Quinn and Santana and Brittany, whether Rachel liked it or not, and if this was the only way they'd come, she owed it to her fellow Gleeks to do right by them.

'It's a deal,' Rachel said, holding her hand out to shake Quinn's. Despite the tiny gold cross hanging around Quinn's neck, Rachel had the feeling she was shaking hands with the devil.

three

Choir room, Monday during lunch period

Rachel had a difficult time concentrating in algebra, even though it was normally easy for her. Instead of focusing on the chalk equations on the blackboard, she was picturing herself onstage, in full *Les Misérables* regalia. Picture a pitch-black stage. The fog (from a fog machine that actually worked, not like the one that ruined the Glee Club performance at the Fall in Love with Music recital last fall) slowly rolls in over the narrow Parisian alleyways. Cue Rachel, in a simple empire-waist peasant dress that manages to actually give her some cleavage. Her mouth opens and the words hang in the air, leaving the audience spellbound. Thunderous applause.

After class, Rachel grabbed her pink insulated lunch

sack from her locker and headed to the choir room. She packed her own lunch most mornings – a sandwich, like today's hummus and turkey in a whole-grain wrap, a Granny Smith apple or a pear, and a plastic Tupperware container of carrots and celery sticks. The hot lunches provided by the school system were practically inedible – artery-clogging mixtures of greasy cheeses and carbohydrates, with nary a vegetable in sight.

The choir room was already half full of Glee students when she arrived. The radiators hissed and spewed hot, dry air into the room. Rachel's eyes immediately fell on Finn, who was sitting on the drum stool and absentmindedly tapping on the gold-plated cymbals. What was it about him that was so . . . charming? In his washed-out blue flannel shirt over a plain white tee, and his faded jeans and black sneakers, he dressed like any other confident, athletic William McKinley High School jock.

But he was so much more than that. It took guts for the most popular guy in school to join Glee Club, something that would normally be complete social suicide. His Neanderthal friends still gave him grief for his affiliation with the nerdy arts kids, but overall, he shook it off like he didn't even care what insults they threw at him. Confidence was a major turn-on for Rachel – it was why she had a brief, ill-fated crush on Alexander Kowalski, the senior lead in *Oklahoma!* her freshman year.

Rachel's mouth opened to say something to Finn – a

question about whether he'd beaten his high score in Grand Theft Auto last night, maybe? Something to appeal to his masculine ego would be perfect. But, before she could, she noticed that Quinn Fabray, sitting in a red plastic chair on the top riser, was staring directly at her, one perfect eyebrow raised as if to say, 'Go for it. Talk to him. Forget our deal.' Santana sat next to her, somehow managing to file her nails, text on her Blackberry, and stare at Rachel with mild disinterest all at the same time.

Rachel quickly walked past Finn without saying a word and threw herself down in the front row, next to Tina and Kurt. 'Thanks for coming,' she couldn't resist saying over her shoulder to Quinn.

'My pleasure.' Quinn's smile was like the Cheshire cat's. She was very pleased with herself. While she didn't love the idea of Finn dating anyone other than her, it was only the thought of him with Rachel that made her physically ill. Anything to keep them far apart – and to torture Rachel in the process – had to be a good thing.

The rest of the Glee kids snuck in the door just as the bell rang. Puck swaggered in, last of all, spinning a basket-ball on his index finger. He gave Quinn a lascivious wink, which she appreciated but promptly ignored. It was their routine, which had been established months ago. He openly hit on her, and she pretended to be uninterested.

'Thank God,' Rachel said, rubbing her hands together with satisfaction. 'We're all here.' She was so excited she almost jumped out of her seat. She couldn't wait to hear which song Mr Schuester wanted her to sing from *Les Mis* – 'I Dreamed a Dream' or 'On My Own'? Those were the ones that would best suit her voice, although she'd be open to discussing other options.

'Except Mr Schu.' Finn stood up and dropped the drumsticks onto a music stand. He yawned. He didn't mind all the secrecy, but he wished he hadn't gotten up half an hour earlier that morning for nothing. He'd been up until three trying – and failing – to shatter his record in Grand Theft Auto IV.

'I'm here. I'm here.' Mr Schuester breezed through the door, a huge grin on his face. With his warm brown eyes that crinkled at the corners and his dark-wash jeans, he didn't look that much older than his students. His leather messenger bag was slung over his shoulder, and he set it down gently on the piano, careful not to scratch the black lacquer. His eyes did a quick scan of the room. 'Thank you, guys, for all being here this time.'

Rachel shot an 'I told you so' look at Quinn.

'So what's the four-one-one?' Mercedes asked, trying not to sound interested. She didn't want, in any way, to associate herself with Rachel, who was practically jumping out of her seat in anticipation.

'The four-one-one is this.' Mr Schuester grabbed a chair and turned it around, then sat down and looked at them over his crossed arms. 'I've been thinking a lot about what sort of performance we could do for the upcoming Multicultural Fair this year.'

'The Multicultural Fair? That actually has a huge audience,' Kurt said optimistically. 'Last year Mr Ryerson wouldn't let us perform because he said the Deer Valley High auditorium had terrible acoustics.' The Multicultural Fair was held every winter at alternating local high schools. It was supposed to be a culmination of each school's celebration of different cultures during Multicultural Week, and it always featured various musical acts – a student mariachi band, a Kabuki theater presentation – along with a buffet dinner with stations devoted to various international cuisines. Last year, at Deer Valley, Kurt met a Deer Valley boy who wore a black Chanel scarf around his head as he served jalapeño enchiladas. This year was McKinley's turn to host – maybe enchilada boy would come to him.

'Well, this year we're going to take advantage of the Multicultural Fair to do something a little different.' Mr Schuester pulled a photograph from his satchel and held it up for everyone to see. A very skinny-looking Will Schuester in a McKinley High sweatshirt had his arm around a tall, handsome teenager in a black turtleneck.

'Are you trying to tell us you're gay, Mr Schu?' Puck glanced nervously at Kurt. If there was another gay guy in Glee Club, Puck was going to have a hard time convincing the basketball dudes that there wasn't something suspicious going on.

Kurt rolled his eyes. Puck was the worst of the Neanderthals, despite his stirring rendition of 'Sweet Caroline' and his impossibly tight biceps.

'When is that? 1985?' Santana asked, squinting at the photo.

'This was 1994,' Mr Schuester corrected. He shot a stern look in Puck's direction, but Puck was staring down at his chest, trying to see if the weight-training workout he'd squeezed in that morning was showing any results yet. 'This is my friend Philippe, who was a French exchange student my family hosted during my junior year. We had a really great time getting to know each other and learning about each other's cultures, and Philippe especially loved hanging out with the McKinley High Glee Club because he didn't have anything like it back at his school in France.'

Rachel pressed her lips together. She knew that Glee had seen a golden era in Mr Schu's time – the dozens of trophies and plaques in the trophy case across from the auditorium reminded them every time they went to practice. Each time she saw them, she thought how lucky Mr Schuester had been to belong to the high school's Glee Club before slushies were used as weapons and when people with talent were actually admired instead of ridiculed. But part of her also kind of resented that Glee had been so successful then – why not now? What was so much better about 1994? 'It's all very interesting when you share your personal history with us and all, Mr Schuester, but how is this going to help us win at regionals?'

'Hold on, Rachel.' Mr Schuester sighed. Rachel could practically hear him think *This isn't about you*, but he held his tongue. Despite his constant need to assert his authority over her, they both knew she was the key to Glee's revival. 'As I was saying, Philippe was so impressed with our Glee Club, it inspired him to start his own back in France.'

'Boring. I'm bored now,' Puck muttered under his breath, leaning back in his chair and trying to see up Santana's skirt. He preferred it when the girls wore the cheerleading uniforms without the leggings underneath, but he still couldn't help peeking.

Mr Schuester didn't hear him. 'We've managed to keep in touch over the years, and now Philippe teaches at a high school in Lyon and runs his school's glee club.' He paused for effect. 'And get this: they're all coming to visit McKinley – just in time to perform with us at the multi-cultural festivities!'

The room immediately came alive. This was definitely good news. Life in Lima, Ohio, was not terribly exciting, especially in the middle of winter. An influx of foreign teenagers – and glee club-loving ones at that – would stir things up. Everyone was grinning, and a few of the kids were pulling out their phones to text their friends or update their statuses.

'European chicks? Hot.' Puck leaned forward in his seat, suddenly paying attention. 'You know, they're much more open minded over there.' He'd seen *National Lampoon's European Vacation*. Maybe he'd had enough of repressed American girls who held their V-cards under lock and key.

'Is it too late to ask them to bring some Louis Vuitton over? It's so much cheaper when you buy direct.' Kurt's eyes widened. He was desperate for a new garment bag. He was already planning his outfits in case Glee Club made it to nationals.

'They're arriving tomorrow – and I would love for you all to come up with some sort of welcome number to perform for them.' Mr Schuester still couldn't believe that, starting tomorrow, his kids would have the chance to experience something like he had when he was their age. It had blown his mind to meet Philippe and the other kids in the French exchange, who lived in a world so far away from Lima, Ohio. It was amazing to talk about the things that were totally different – how Philippe had been sipping wine at the dinner table since he was eight, for example – as well as the things they shared, like a love for music. 'Something to show them what you've got before we get started rehearsing for our joint performance.'

Rachel's hand shot into the air, almost poking Tina in the eye. 'I volunteer to lead the project.' Even though no one objected, she took a defensive posture. 'After all, I don't think it's a shock to say that I'm the most worldly and sophisticated of us all, and I have a very European mindset.' While she was slightly disappointed that she wasn't going to be singing her very own *Les Mis* solo, the prospect of meeting new people – French ones! – and wowing them with her incredible talent was pretty exciting.

'What makes you so worldly?' Kurt asked, leaning forward in his chair. If she mentioned the talent competition she'd won in Cleveland when she was three, he was going to throw a stack of show-tune sheet music at her, and it was heavy.

'To start with, I've been to France.' Rachel raised her nose in the air. Most of the kids at McKinley High, with the exception of rich kids, had never been out of the country, much less to Europe. 'My dads took me there when I was nine months old, so I've seen the Eiffel Tower, even if I don't remember it.'

'I think that Rachel leading the group on this one is a great idea,' Quinn spoke up, her voice as smooth as honey. Everyone else was nodding in agreement. One of the good things about Rachel was that she was always willing to do the work to put something together, mainly because it stroked her ego to feel in charge. And Quinn was all for Rachel keeping busy – and keeping her hands off Finn.

Quinn's hazel eyes settled on Finn. He was now pouring a bag of chips into his open mouth. A few crumbs landed on one of the drums. He was gross sometimes, but no grosser than other boys, and he was still incredibly handsome. Quinn felt a pang in her stomach. It really was a shame that Puck was the father instead of Finn. They'd been so perfect together, in so many ways. The head cheerleader and the quarterback of the football team (now, the star forward of the basketball team) – it was exactly what every other girl on the planet dreamed about when she lay in bed at night. But that was all in the past now.

Maybe Quinn shouldn't have lied to him about the baby – even if she did it because she was terrified and didn't know what else to do. Not only had she broken the vow she took as president of the Celibacy Club, but she had cheated on her boyfriend in a moment of lusty weakness to do it. She really missed Finn. Things between them had been cemented into place at the homecoming dance, and for the months following that, they'd been exactly that adorable couple who made everyone else green with envy. Even when Quinn's scandalous pregnancy had been revealed to the McKinley student body, Finn had stood by her and taken responsibility like a real man. Finn's mom had even caught him serenading the sonogram photo Quinn had sent him of the baby. Amazingly, through all of it, Quinn still fantasized about bad-boy Puck, and it felt like Finn held part of himself away from her, like he knew deep down that something was off.

Then, after Finn discovered her terrible secret before

sectionals, he and Rachel began spending a lot of time together. Quinn knew that she had no chance of fixing things between her and Finn at the time. It seemed like Finn and Rachel started dating almost immediately, although, mercifully, the relationship didn't last, probably because Finn realized it wasn't that much fun to date a girl with man hands, even if she knew how to sing.

Maybe it was childish of Quinn to try to keep Rachel away from Finn, but she didn't care. There was just something about Rachel – like how she acted all superior just because she was talented – that drove Quinn crazy. If Rachel wanted to date someone, it should be her social equal – someone like Artie, or that annoying J-Fro kid who was always snooping around, trying to gather gossip for his blog.

But whatever. Rachel, who was surrounded by some of the Glee kids and talking in her annoying loud voice about their French visitors, was keeping her eyes off Finn.

Perfect.

four

Mr Horn's English class, Monday, last period

The heating systems at McKinley High hadn't been updated since the building was built. Consequently, most of the rooms during the winter were either absolutely freezing or unbearably hot. In the English wing, the classrooms were the latter, and the saunalike feeling in the rooms made it even harder to concentrate. Ten minutes before the end of Mr Horn's last-period English class, most students were already surreptitiously stuffing their notebooks into their backpacks. No disrespect was meant to Mr Horn, who was a decent teacher, but Mondays were always excruciating and the last few minutes felt like hours. With the end of the school day so close, the students could practically smell it, and attention spans usually went from small to minuscule. Puck, hiding his phone in his lap, was sending dirty texts to Santana, and Brittany was reading a magazine, out in the open, as if Mr Horn would be proud she was simply reading at all.

Artie was one of the few students in class paying attention. He thought Mr Horn was brilliant. He'd gone to UC Berkeley as an undergrad, and he had an uncanny ability to make things like *Heart of Darkness* by Joseph Conrad, a book that had made Artie want to pull his hair out, come alive when he spent an entire class period showing clips from *Lost*. He had his notebook open, jotting down notes as Mr Horn wrapped up the discussion of *Macbeth*. He even wrote down a question or two to ask him after class. Artie had managed to get As in all his classes since he was a freshman, but it was English and French that he liked best. He'd even started taking Spanish this year, since Romance languages seemed to come easily to him.

'Brittany, save me some self-respect and put your magazine away.' Mr Horn sighed, drumming his fingers on a stack of papers. 'The school day isn't over yet.'

'Sorry, Mr Horn.' Brittany carefully closed the magazine, keeping a finger on her page, which featured new belts for spring. 'It's only, like, three minutes.'

'Exactly, we still have three minutes. We can get plenty done in this time.' Mr Horn turned toward the blackboard, above which hung a series of theater posters – *As You Like*

It, Six Characters in Search of an Author, The Crucible. 'Like, I give you your homework assignment.'

The class groaned in unison.

Mr Horn handed copies of a small paperback book to the first person in each row and asked them to pass them back. Mayur Deshmukh, the tall guy who sat in front of Artie and always smelled like burnt popcorn, let the books fall on Artie's desk carelessly. Before Artie could grab them, they slid to the floor.

Mayur glanced back. 'Oh, dude. Sorry.' He quickly picked the books off the floor, handed one to Artie, and passed the rest to the girl behind him.

Mr Horn erased the blackboard, which had been covered with his all-caps handwriting. 'Tonight, I'd like you to read the first half of *Cyrano de Bergerac*, a play by Edmond Rostand. And I really think you're going to like it. It's about an intelligent poet and musician – a romantic, thoughtful man – who also happens to have a serious physical disability.'

Artie blinked. He was intrigued. He didn't see too many physically disabled people in books, or on TV, or in movies. But that didn't mean they weren't out there. He flipped through the book, a faded yellow paperback with creased pages and underlined passages. His eyes caught on to the first page he came to: *god's whiskers! Your face is hideous as the demons in my storybook!* At the side of the page, there was an ink drawing of a man standing at the edge

45

of the room, lurking in the shadows, hiding his face in his shoulder as he watched an elaborate ball go on around him.

After spending his whole life – well, his whole life since age eight, when Artie was in the car accident that left him paralyzed from the waist down – feeling like he was hiding in the shadows, watching, he thought that maybe this play was for him. Maybe others, when they read it, would realize how it felt to be someone whose body kept him from ever fitting in.

Even though Artie would give anything to have just a big nose to worry about.

'And I'm assuming none of you will have a problem handing in a three-page paper by Friday,' Mr Horn said.

Artie glanced over his shoulder. Across the aisle, Puck was doing that weird sleeping-with-his-eyes-open thing that Artie had to admire – you could tell he was sleeping only when you noticed that he wasn't blinking. Behind him, Brittany was doodling prom dresses. He couldn't count on them to get anything out of the reading. They could barely read.

'Also,' Mr Horn continued, 'since I still have you for two more minutes, there should be plenty of time to hand back your midterm papers.'

Another collective groan from the class startled Puck awake. He sat up straighter, ran a hand over his Mohawk, and nodded at a girl across the room who'd been glancing at him. 'Whassup,' he said in his trademark half-sneer before returning to his napping pose like a startled dog drifting back to sleep.

Artie rolled his eyes. He'd never figure out why Puck was such a lothario. Sure, he had the attributes that shallower members of the female species might value – status as a full-fledged, three-varsity-sport jock, confident Kanye West swagger, well-defined biceps – but Artie didn't get why even girls who seemed like they should know better fell for his macho routine. Really, Puck was just a giant bully with a low IQ who liked to make fart jokes and talk about Super Mario Brothers. Maybe it was some kind of animal instinct thing, like the way the female lions were attracted to the biggest lions with the loudest roars, the ones who ran around attacking the slightly weaker lions who were just minding their own business.

Needless to say, Artie had not forgiven Puck for locking him in the janitor's closet last year. Artie had had to call the front office from his cell phone, in the dark because he couldn't reach the light switch, to let him out. Mrs Goodrich, Principal Figgins's secretary, had hung up on him once because she'd thought it was a crank call.

'Some of you really seemed to understand Holden Caulfield.' Mr Horn slipped Artie's paper down on his desk. An *A+* was written in red ink across the top next to a smiley face. Artie grinned.

Mr Horn handed Brittany and Puck their papers. 'And

some of you . . . didn't.' Both had giant *F*s, each accompanied by a frowny face. Brittany stuffed her paper into her magazine. Puck didn't move, having fallen asleep with his eyes open again.

Mr Horn looked down at Puck. 'I hope that gives you something to think about, Noah.' To an untrained eye, Puck did look like he was deep in thought, perhaps pondering his future as a burger flipper in Lima, Ohio.

The bell rang, sending students jumping to their feet while stuffing their papers into their backpacks and gathering the rest of their belongings. Puck didn't move, so Artie gave him a quick poke in the shoulder as he rolled by him.

Puck startled awake. In his white thermal long-sleeve tee under a flannel shirt with the sleeves ripped off, he looked exactly like the kind of guy who would lock someone in a janitor's closet. 'I was just letting you know that class is over,' Artie said quickly.

'Oh. Thanks, dude.' Puck stood up and stretched. *There is nothing like a nap at the end of the day to make me feel good.* He'd had an amazing dream in which he was stranded on a tropical island with a girls' beach volleyball team.

'Are you going to practice?' Artie asked, curious if Puck was going to bail again. It felt weird to talk about 'practice' with a jock and mean Glee practice. Puck had joined Glee about a month after Mr Schuester had taken over, mostly,

Artie suspected, to try to get with Santana or Brittany, the two Cheerios who, along with Quinn, had joined the original core group of Kurt, Mercedes, Rachel, Tina, and Artie. Also, once Finn had agreed to be part of Glee, a few other football guys followed, significantly increasing the toughness quotient of the club. He knew Puck liked being in Glee Club, even if he didn't always show up on time. Artie figured his tardiness was some kind of self-conscious, bad-boy type of thing.

'What am I, your girlfriend?' Puck scowled at Artie and barely glanced at the F paper on his desk before he stuffed it into his back pocket. He grabbed his backpack. 'Yeah, I'm going to practice. Just don't, you know, wheel too close to me.'

Artie noticed that Puck had left his copy of *Cyrano* on his desk. 'Hey, you forgot your homework.'

Puck grinned and jammed the book into his backpack. 'Dude, I haven't done a reading assignment in two years.'

Obviously, Artie thought. Even though Puck walked several feet away from him through the hallways, Artie could feel the benefits of his presence. Girls loved Puck, and guys were terrified of him. Almost everyone gave Artie a glance, something he wasn't used to. It was much more normal for people to pretend not to see him.

When they got to the choir room, Rachel was sitting on the piano bench. She jumped up at the sight of them. 'Finally,' she said accusingly, her brown eyes resting on

Artie, as if he'd somehow slowed them down. 'We've been waiting for you!'

'The bell rang approximately three minutes ago!' Artie exclaimed, pushing his chair over to where Tina was sitting, a sketchbook propped open on her lap. Kurt was sitting on the other side of her, watching a YouTube video of a spring fashion show on his phone. Brittany and Santana were in the back, practicing some dance steps. Finn gave Puck a high five for an unspecified reason, and everyone turned to look at Rachel, who, whenever Mr Schuester wasn't there, became the de facto leader of the club.

'You're probably all dying to know what sort of wonderful number I've managed to come up with for you in the few short hours since we last met.' Rachel rubbed her hands together in anticipation. 'So I won't keep you waiting any longer.' Several brown paper bags were lined up at her feet. She reached into the first one and pulled out a handful of black-and-white-striped shirts. She tossed them toward Kurt, who quickly passed them around. Then she tore into the next bag and started tossing brightly colored berets like Frisbees at the other kids. When she got to the last one, she perched it jauntily on her head. 'Can you say "Lady Marmalade", anyone?'

Mercedes held her purple beret out in front of her like it was diseased. 'You know this is kind of a stereotype, don't you? I mean, French people don't really dress like this.'

Rachel straightened her shoulders. She was a team player and believed in the First Amendment and all, but sometimes she just knew more than others did and it would greatly benefit everyone if they just trusted her. 'That's not true. The song selection is contemporary, and the outfits are traditional French . . .'

'I don't know, Rachel.' Finn held the black-and-white-striped T-shirt against his chest awkwardly. The red beret on his head made him look slightly clownish. 'I feel like one of those mime guys. What do you think?'

Rachel deliberately refrained from answering Finn, and there was only a brief moment of awkward silence before a few other voices jumped in to express their reservations.

'Do you really think that's an appropriate song?' Artie asked, spinning his beret awkwardly on his index finger. 'The chorus is basically saying . . .'

'Look, if you know another French song that would offer such an opportunity for a wide range of vocal expression, please, suggest it now.' Rachel planted her hands firmly on her hips and stared down Artie, who simply shrugged his shoulders. 'I didn't think so.'

'But . . .' Mercedes started.

'Who here has been to France? Anyone? Anyone besides me?' Rachel nearly shouted down Mercedes. She smiled, satisfied, when no one answered. She may have been not-yet-one when her dads took her there, but she'd always been an impressionable youth and she was certain the

French culture had seeped through her baby skin. She was careful not to look at Finn as she spoke because Quinn's hawk eyes were on her, and she was pretty sure, by way of their agreement, she wasn't even supposed to speak to Finn in a group setting. Why had she agreed to this stupid deal, anyway?

'I think it's a great idea.' Mr Schuester walked into the room, his leather messenger bag stuffed with papers. 'I'm sorry I'm late, everyone. But I completely agree with Rachel.' He looked almost surprised as he said the words. '"Lady Marmalade" is an excellent choice.'

Quinn raised her hand but spoke up before anyone could call on her. 'Rachel, when did you have time to go off campus and buy such fantastic outfits?' Quinn was dying to bust Rachel for something – anything – and if she knew Rachel was sneaking off campus, maybe Rachel wouldn't be able to blackmail her into coming to every single Glee meeting anymore. Quinn deserved a little slack for what she was currently going through, and Rachel deserved a little taste of her own bitter medicine.

'Actually, the berets are mine,' Kurt said. A navy blue beret was perched neatly on his head, and it looked strikingly natural on him. 'Rachel texted me during my independent study period and explained that there was a costume emergency. Luckily, I have a nice collection of berets as they were very in last spring.'

'Wait, berets are in? Like the cheese?' Brittany whispered to Santana. 'I totally missed that.'

'That's Brie, not berets,' Santana whispered back.

Quinn narrowed her eyes. 'And the T-shirts?' She sniffed hers. It smelled vaguely like basement.

'I borrowed them from Madame Dimmig, the French teacher,' Rachel explained. *Nice try, Quinn*, Rachel thought. 'The French department put on a juggling performance at last year's Multicultural Fair, and everyone dressed up as mimes.'

'See!' Finn stood up. 'I told you these were mime costumes.'

Rachel bit her lip. Finn was looking directly at her, and he was going to think she was a horrible person if she kept ignoring his comments. This was a terrible deal. The only good thing about it was that Quinn and the Cheerios were here, ready to rehearse the new number. It was going to be complicated, and they had only a little time to get it ready for the performance in front of the French kids tomorrow, so she needed their full cooperation. She glanced at Finn, whose hair had grown longer over the past few months and was kind of flopping down over his forehead in this way that made Rachel want to push it out of his eyes.

Why was Finn the price she had to pay?

Across the room, Quinn was still watching her. Maybe she hadn't busted Little Miss Perfect for skipping class, but still, it was very satisfying to watch Rachel almost trip over herself each time she realized she couldn't talk to Finn. It served her right for being so bossy and micro-managing.

Mr Schuester handed everyone copies of the sheet music. He knew the best way to avoid further drama was to just get his kids doing what they liked best – singing. 'Let's take it from the top!'

five

McKinley High cafeteria, Tuesday lunch

I n honor of Multicultural Week, the underpaid kitchen staff members at William McKinley High were given the added duty of decorating the cafeteria each morning before lunch with themed decorations. Tuesday was Mexican Day. The yellow walls of the cafeteria were strung with brightly colored sombreros, and hanging temptingly from the ceiling fixtures were a half dozen old piñatas, undoubtedly dug out from the supplies room in the basement. They were too high for the students to realistically swing anything at, but several enterprising students had stood on chairs and tossed their notebooks toward them, hoping to break them and shower the room with candies that weren't actually there.

The dining services supervisor was friends with the owner of Aztec's, a small chain of Mexican restaurants in western Ohio, and had purchased, at a steep discount, several vats of the *queso* sauce Aztec's was famous for. It was getting worked into the burritos, poured over the enchiladas and the chile rellenos, and drizzled across the nachos. The beefy football players (the students who were thought of as football players even when the season was over and they had turned to basketball instead) kept rushing back in line for seconds and thirds, and even the Cheerios, who were on strict diet and exercise regimens designed for them personally by Coach Sylvester, were enjoying the cuisine, although more sparingly.

Kurt neatly cut up his *queso*-infused bean burrito with his knife and fork as he watched Quinn steal a nacho off Finn's plate. The popular kids got the best tables in the cafeteria – the ones overlooking the courtyard, which, at this time of year, was covered in pristine white snowdrifts. The picnic tables outside, which would become hot property when the weather warmed up, were unrecognizable under the two feet of snow the past weeks' storms dropped on the state. 'Why do they still sit together, if they're not going out anymore?'

Kurt was sitting with his everyday lunch companions – Mercedes, Artie, and Tina – at a round table more toward the corner of the room. Rachel usually honored them with her presence, as well, though today she said she'd just brought an apple and a protein bar because she never ate a large meal before a performance. The French students were due to arrive sometime soon, and the Glee kids were psyched to see some new faces in town. Kurt, however, still liked Finn's face best of all.

'Popularity trumps love,' Artie suggested, wiping his hands on a crumpled-up napkin. The burritos were out of this world. 'You can't have the popular crowd fracture just because the king and queen broke up.'

'I'm tired of talking about Quinn and Finn,' Mercedes announced. She had on a T-shirt with a picture of Michael Jackson in his red leather jacket and a gold necklace that spelled her name. 'They're not the only people in this world.'

'What about the French kids who are coming?' Tina asked, propping her heavy combat boots up on an empty chair. 'Do you think they'll be nice?'

Mercedes rubbed her hands together and smiled wickedly. She'd already eaten her first burrito and was considering going back for another. 'Who cares if they're nice? Do you think there's going to be any hotties? We could use some new blood.'

'God, I hope so.' Kurt touched his carefully sprayed hair. 'I'm hoping they look like they came from a Truffaut movie.' Truffaut was his favorite foreign film director, and the people in his gorgeous black-and-white movies were so elegant and perfect that they almost didn't look human.

'I just hope they're friendly.' Tina stared at her plate and swirled the last bit of her enchilada around in the sauce. She glanced at Artie. She had no idea what was going on with him anymore. He'd been acting distant lately, and every time Tina asked him what was up, he pretended nothing was wrong, so she let it go. It was sad, but if he kept on pushing her away, it must be because he'd rather not be with her.

'Do you think they're going to be really good singers?' Artie asked, taking a sip from his can of orange soda. One day, he'd like to go to Paris, although he didn't know if the Eiffel Tower was handicapped-accessible. It had to have an elevator, right? People couldn't walk all the way to the top.

'I don't know.' Mercedes shook her head. She wanted them to be *good* singers, but not *great*. Definitely not better than the Glee members were – there was already too much ego in the choir room – though Mercedes kind of hoped the French kids would put on an incredible rendition of something from *Les Mis*, just to show up Rachel, who never stopped blabbing about her favorite musical. 'They certainly can't have all the "extensive vocal training" that *some* of us have,' she said, repeating one of Rachel's favorite phrases.

Puck, whose empty tray of food was covered with crumpled napkins, stopped as he walked by. 'Whatever the Frenchies are like, you can be sure that all the girls will want a taste of the Puckster.' He felt only a tiny twinge of guilt as he realized he'd said it loud enough for Quinn, who was returning from the food line with a mini carton of skim milk, to hear him as she passed.

Quinn heard him, of course, but she ignored him, continuing her conversation with Santana about how long she'd have to work out that afternoon to burn off the calories in the enchiladas. Quinn normally ate only salads at lunch, but the Mexican food had smelled so delicious, she couldn't resist. Luckily, eating whatever she wanted without feeling any residual guilt was the one perk to being pregnant. It was a welcome change from her old routine of just chewing ice for lunch back in her Cheerios days.

Quinn didn't bat an eyelash at Puck's stupid bragging. It was nothing new – he loved to try to provoke her, like he was hoping it would get her to hook up with him again. Ever since their secret affair, there was still an underlying current of energy between them, especially when Quinn was still dating Finn, and even now, when she was single. But it just wasn't going to happen between them – baby or not.

'Forty-five minutes. At least,' Quinn announced definitively.

'Maybe if I do interval training. I say an hour on the treadmill, easily.' Santana twisted the cap off her bottle of water.

Quinn tossed her blond hair over her shoulder, knowing that Puck was probably watching her walk away. It was definitely a game of cat and mouse between them, but she was never sure exactly which of them was the cat. Sometimes she thought of earth science class freshman year, when Mr Papagni had shown how two repelling magnets, when flipped around, could become stuck to each other.

'Puck is seriously a man-slut,' Santana commented, popping a piece of spearmint gum into her mouth. She offered the pack to Quinn, who declined. 'He needs to tone it down. Shouldn't he, like, lay low after knocking you up?'

Quinn just smiled sweetly as she slid back into her seat. Santana wasn't quite over Puck, despite having moved on with Ryan Taylor, the center on the basketball team. Quinn thought Santana would be more angry with her when she found out what had gone on between her and Puck, but their relationship hadn't changed all that much. Maybe Santana was happy that Quinn had left the spot of head Cheerio vacant, or maybe she was just relieved that she wasn't the one who'd ended up pregnant (to everyone's surprise, including her own). But despite recent events, Santana was still clearly attracted to Puck. Quinn sighed. 'He can't help himself. He was cursed with too much testosterone.'

'Did I tell you what Coach Sylvester said about my

thighs yesterday?' Santana glanced down at her thin yet muscular legs. 'She said they looked like two elephant seals in a ritual mating fight. I so should have passed on that *queso*.'

'Uh-oh. Looks like the show's on.' Across the table, Finn, who was taller than everyone in the lunchroom, spotted Mr Schuester coming through the door. He clapped his hands when he saw his Glee kids, stopping first at the table where Artie and Kurt sat. 'Mr Schu's here.'

'It's time to get ready, guys. Philippe's club will be arriving at McKinley any minute.' Mr Schuester clamped his hand on Artie's shoulder for a few seconds before letting go. His face was flushed with excitement, and his curly hair seemed to stand up even more than normal.

'We're on, Mr Schu.' Kurt grabbed his tray and stood up. After all that time collecting berets, they were finally going to be put to good use. It was a fashionista's version of being environmentally friendly: reduce, *reuse*, recycle.

six

Choir room, Tuesday afternoon

'I feel like that old guy on the Get Out of Jail Free cards in Monopoly,' Puck announced, pulling his tight striped T-shirt away from his chest. The shirts fit all of them oddly. They'd paired them with slim-fit black jeans or black skirts, black boots, and, of course, the berets.

'I still feel like a mime.' Artie wrinkled his nose. He wasn't normally too concerned with what he looked like, but he wanted to make a good impression on the French students. 'Or like I should be part of a chain gang.'

'No, you look great, guys.' Mr Schuester had the buoyant, nervous look he always had on his face before a performance. He clearly thrived on pressure and seemed happiest when getting ready for a show, when anything could still happen. He, however, wasn't wearing a beret. 'I'm really impressed with how well you were able to pull this together after just one day. You should all give yourselves a pat on the back.'

They all glanced at one another uneasily. Everything just felt . . . wrong. The radiators in the choir room were spewing hot air, making the space incredibly dry and stuffy. Worse, the smell of Mexican food lingered in the hallways and had seeped into the room. It had smelled delicious before lunch, but after eating it, the smell made them all nauseated. And then there were the problems with the outfits. The T-shirts weren't identical, and each one had little flourishes that Kurt had added during his study hall to 'glam up' the performance. Artie's shirt had a fleur-de-lis BeDazzled on the sleeve, and Tina's shirt had a necklace of fake pearls sewn into the fabric at the neckline.

'It's just butterflies,' Mr Schuester announced, taking in the nervous expressions on their faces. 'But trust me, guys, you can nail this.'

'I just feel . . . funny,' Quinn murmured, rubbing her stomach. The butterflies were more like a flock of pigeons, and they were flapping their wings as if they were trying to fly to China. In fact, several other students looked as unsettled as she felt, so it couldn't have been leftover morning sickness. And why was the room so hot? Outside, the white snow, glittering in the sunshine, made Quinn want to dive into it.

Finn glanced at Rachel. Her striped shirt had a wide scoop neck and showed off her shoulders. She had on a pleated black skirt that spun around her when she moved. Finn never knew where she got so many skirts like that, but he liked them. He was used to some preperformance chatter with her to calm her nerves – she'd usually talk about how Quinn was always sharp, or how if only Kurt could remember the moves, he'd be great – but she wasn't even looking at him. He didn't know what was up with her – maybe it was something with the French kids. Rachel got nervous when she thought about anyone stealing her thunder. But it was totally uncharacteristic of her to be so silent.

'You ready for this?' Finn asked her, a little awkwardly, because she wasn't exactly looking at him.

Rachel jumped. She looked at him for a second with a panicked expression in her brown eyes. But when she opened her mouth, she just hummed, 'Mum mum mum mum mum.' Then she turned and walked away.

Finn looked down at himself. He knew Rachel was serious about her vocal warm-ups, but that was weird. Maybe it was because he looked ridiculous in his too-tight shirt with the word GLAM embroidered in cursive down one sleeve. He held the red beret in his hands, wishing that he didn't have to be seen dressed like that. He hoped none of the French girls were too hot.

'Don't worry, guys.' Mr Schuester had his game face on

and was almost dancing in excitement. He'd straightened up the room, erased the dirty cartoon someone had drawn on the blackboard, and polished the piano with the special chamois cloth that was stored in the piano bench. 'I know you're not too rehearsed on this number, but you sounded great yesterday.'

'I don't feel good,' Brittany said under her breath to Santana. She tugged at the collar of her turtleneck, pulling it away from her skin. 'I feel like I'm about to become bulimic.'

'Suck it up,' Santana hissed, though she didn't really feel any better. She walked over to the windows, unlocked one, and pushed it open six inches. A burst of cold air rushed into the room. 'They're coming!'

The Glee kids got to their feet. A tall, lanky man in trendy black-framed glasses walked through the door, nodding slowly as he took everything in. Behind him trailed the students in his club, and the Glee kids tried not to stare. Mr Schuester's face burst into a grin. 'Philippe! *Bienvenue à* McKinley High!' Suddenly, there was a rush of cheek kisses and patting on the back as the two teachers greeted each other for the first time in years. Kurt watched in admiration. He wished Americans would kiss each other hello like that. It was so sophisticated, and it would give him a chance to smell Finn's aftershave up close.

'Guys, this is Monsieur Philippe Renaud, and this is his glee club from Lycée de Lyon, all the way from Lyon,

France.' Mr Schuester waved his hands with a flourish toward the new students.

Monsieur Renaud nodded humbly as he adjusted his glasses. In his slate-gray shirt and dark pants, he looked like a J.Crew model. *Did they have J.Crew in France?* Kurt wondered. 'It is an honor to be here again.' He spoke with a slight French accent that made the girls in Glee shiver.

'Hot,' Santana whispered to Brittany, forgetting about her stomach pains.

'Totally,' Brittany whispered back, adjusting her ponytail. *Is it wrong to want to make out with a teacher? Maybe it is okay when he isn't* your *teacher?*

'And this is the Lycée de Lyon Chorale, or, as you like to call it, glee club.' Monsieur Renaud's handsome chin lifted slightly as he went down the line, introducing each of his students. 'This is Jean-Paul.' A tall, moody-looking guy dressed in all black with chin-length dark hair. 'Celeste.' A slim girl with gorgeous blond Taylor Swift-like curls that cascaded over her shoulders. All the boys – except Kurt – leaned forward in their chairs. 'Rielle.' Another cute girl with pixieish hair, a T-shirt with the name of a French band, and a pair of knee-high leather boots. 'Gerard.' A short but stocky boy who flexed his biceps when Mr Renaud introduced him. 'Angelique, Marc, Claire, Nicholas, Aimee and Sophie.'

Artie was a little shocked. He'd expected all the French students to be tall and lean and unbearably sophisticated, and while there definitely were some beautiful people in the club, there were some nerdy-looking kids as well. One of the guys – named Nicholas, maybe? – was on the pudgy side, and another guy wore a T-shirt with an Asterix cartoon that looked too brand-new to be ironic. It seemed that nerdiness was something that transcended culture.

Everyone else, though, was staring at Celeste, who looked sleek and tall in a pair of jeans, a plain white T-shirt, and a black fitted blazer with the sleeves rolled up. The second-most intriguing exchange student was Rielle, who had a guitar strapped to her back. Everyone liked a girl who could play guitar.

In her chair against the wall, Quinn fidgeted uncomfortably. She had always hated girls who were prettier than she was. There weren't many of them at McKinley High, and until recently, she didn't consider any of them a viable threat. She couldn't help but feel that any day now, her former admirers wouldn't even glance her way, unless it was to gawk at her pregnant belly. She could come to terms with this fact, but she did not like the way Finn was giving his goofy smile to that blond girl. Quinn knew how he felt about Taylor Swift. He'd probably forgotten that he was wearing an über-dorky black-and-white-striped shirt.

Mr Schuester cleared his throat. 'Everyone, I just want to say how happy I am that we're all together. I'm sure this is going to be a valuable learning experience for both parties, culturally and musically.' He looked at the French kids. He knew European teenagers spoke foreign languages much better than their American counterparts, so he didn't want to talk too slowly and insult them. 'I'm really excited for us all to collaborate on a number while you're here in the States. But in the meantime, I'd like you to sit back and enjoy a performance we put together for you.'

The French kids took their seats as the Glee Club kids lined up in front of the piano and tried to ignore the uncomfortable feelings in their stomachs. Rachel hoped the French students hadn't prepared a performance for them as well, because she wasn't prepared to deal with it if any of them was more talented than she was.

The piano player started the music to 'Lady Marmalade'. Mercedes had the first solo. '*Hey, sister, go, sister,*' she started to sing, although Rachel could tell her heart wasn't completely into it. Strange. Because Mercedes was so jealous of Rachel's star status, she usually went all out when she sang to try to prove she was diva material, too. Maybe Mercedes was just feeling lazy. Rachel *knew* she should have taken the first solo. Oh well. She could see the faces of the French kids, and they were all nodding along with smiles on their faces. In fact, they looked fairly entertained.

Then as soon as Mercedes's solo was almost done, Tina rushed out of the room, her black boots making a disturbing amount of noise against the linoleum floor.

Rachel scowled. That was not very professional of Tina. She'd never been a great dancer, but usually she knew that the steps didn't involve taking her out of the room.

Then they came to the first chorus of '*Voulez-vous coucher avec moi*', and Brittany, midstep, dashed out of the room holding her mouth. *Okaaaay . . . that's weird*, Rachel thought as she sang a little louder to compensate.

Mr Schuester, sitting in the front row, looked mystified. *What the hell is going on? Is this some kind of joke?* But then, three seconds later, Puck dashed out of the room, clutching his stomach. Almost immediately, Kurt followed him, and one by one, the rest of the Glee kids, with the exception of Rachel, fled the room.

Rachel stood in the middle of the room, singing the chorus by herself. Part of her wondered if this was some kind of prank the others were pulling on her. Not that she minded having a huge solo – but this was too strange. Nevertheless, she knew that a true performer makes the best of any situation, and she gave one hundred and ten percent to the performance, just like she always did, dancing across the open floor space and meeting the eyes of all the French kids. When the song ended, she gave a slight bow.

There was a smattering of polite applause. The French kids looked back and forth at one another, trying not to giggle. It was really weird that part of the act involved the whole group, except for one girl, running out of the room. It also seemed funny that the pretty girl with the dark brown hair was singing French words to them – words that translated to 'Will you sleep with me tonight?' With her pleated black skirt and white kneesocks that had pink bows on them, it seemed faintly ironic, though she'd sung the song with such eagerness, like she really meant it. Maybe the rumors they'd heard that Americans were very sexually forward – and also blunt – were actually true. That one blond girl also looked as if she might be pregnant. Was that part of the joke? Funny Americans.

'Excuse me, Philippe.' Mr Schuester got to his feet. There was an apologetic smile on his face. After all their work, this was the performance they'd made their first impression with? 'I've got to go see what's going on with my kids. Rachel, would you please, um, entertain the Lycée de Lyon group?'

Rachel beamed. 'Of course.' She wished she'd be asked to 'entertain' people every day. 'I just have to tell you, I believe *Les Misérables* is one of the most perfect musicals in the world.'

A few kids snickered under their breath, but not loud enough for Rachel to notice. The blond girl with the ridiculously beautiful hair – Celeste? – spoke up, her voice tentative but her English quite accomplished. 'I actually love the American musical *West Side Story*.'

Rachel's brown eyes widened. 'It's also my favorite.' A discussion of musical theater quickly followed, with several of the French kids jumping in about what their dream parts would be. Rachel was pleased to find the French kids so friendly, though she was slightly bothered by the fact that Celeste thought the role of Maria in *West Side Story* was 'made for her'. Maybe it was her inexpert English, but Rachel knew that if the role of Maria was 'made for' anyone, it was Rachel Berry. She was too polite to point this out, however.

A few minutes later, Mr Schuester returned to the room, a chagrined look on his face. He was all alone. 'Everyone, I'm so sorry about that. It looks like everyone is feeling a little . . . unsettled . . . due to some bad Mexican food at lunch today.'

The girls made faces. Rachel wasn't terribly surprised. When you looked at a plate of cafeteria food and couldn't identify whether it had come from a plant or an animal, it was a bad sign. During freshman year she'd started a petition to demand that the cafeteria offer at least one vegetarian selection every day, and only two people had signed it. One of them was Jacob, who had asked her if it was true that eating green vegetables made girls horny. She threw out the petition after that.

Mr Schuester grabbed his leather bag from the table and extracted a sheet of paper from it. With a piece of Scotch tape, he posted it in the middle of the blackboard. 'This is a list of names – Monsieur Renaud and I have paired up each French exchange student with an American student who will show our visitors around McKinley High over the next week. You can rely on your American partners to guide you, teach you about American high school life – I'm sure they'll all be feeling better tomorrow. Basically, they'll be your mentors and friends up until the big Multicultural Week performance.'

Again, Rachel beamed. She felt a little funny being the only American in the room for Mr Schuester's speech, but she was proud to represent her country. It was just too bad that the Lyon kids had to have such a gross first impression of McKinley High.

Mr Schuester smiled weakly, hoping the other kids would make it out of the bathrooms soon. He was going to have a few words with dining services for making his kids so ill. He really wanted to have his students spend some time with their partners and get to know one another this afternoon, but now it didn't look like that was going to happen. They were all going to have to work extra hard to recover from the less-than-stellar first impression.

Rachel caught Mr Schuester glancing at the clock. 'I can always perform a quick medley of the songs we've done this year for our French guests, if you like.'

Mr Schuester sighed heavily. Was it wrong of him to regret that out of all the students suffering from food poisoning, Rachel had to be the one exception? 'Rachel, why don't you go check on the girls? Monsieur Renaud and I may have to come up with a new plan for the exchange.'

'Oh.' Rachel didn't let her disappointment show on her face. She was used to Mr Schu getting in her way. He was always trying to keep her down, which didn't make any sense to her, as she was the most talented person who had set foot in the halls of McKinley High since . . . well, since ever.

Instead, she just gave a friendly wave to the French students and said '*Au revoir*' as she walked out the door. It wasn't much of an exit, but it would do for now.

seven

McKinley High hallway, Wednesday morning

Because of the Glee kids' slow recovery from the Mexican food-poisoning fiasco on Tuesday afternoon, Mr Schuester was forced to abandon his plan to introduce each French student to his or her American mentor. Instead, he and Mr Renaud came up with a new and possibly even more fun introduction idea. He gave each French student a picture of his or her American counterpart, photocopied from the William McKinley High School yearbook, and a map marking the location of his or her locker. Mr Schuester believed that this would be an interesting way to introduce the students to one another and hopefully foster some long-lasting friendships between them.

Of course, the best intentions never guarantee success, as Wednesday morning proved. Before first period started, random French students wandered the halls of McKinley with confused looks on their faces, repeatedly being shoved aside by burly basketball players who didn't appreciate anyone standing in their way. Rachel, ever helpful, spotted a few lost students in European-looking clothes and directed them toward the lockers of their mentors. A satisfied smile was on her face as she approached her own locker, eager to meet her match.

A tall, lanky boy – almost all the French kids were thin, which made Rachel wonder what they ate over there – in a black T-shirt and slim-fitting faded black jeans was leaning against Rachel's locker, a bored look on his face. He was watching the American students stream past him, their backpacks overstuffed with textbooks. There was something distinctly European about him, Rachel decided, considering his longish nose and the way his dark hair was pulled into a ponytail at the base of his neck.

'Good morning!' Rachel announced brightly. The boy dragged his eyes away from the crowd to stare at Rachel moodily. His eyes were a startlingly pale blue-gray color. 'You must be Jean-Paul. I'm Rachel Berry, and I'll be your mentor for the rest of your stay here. Welcome to McKinley High!'

The boy didn't respond. Rachel noticed he had two

white cords coming from his ears and disappearing into the back pocket of his jeans. He was listening to an iPod.

Rachel frowned slightly and tapped her finger to one ear, which she hoped was the international sign for 'take out your earphones'. Amazingly, the boy complied, although he took out only the left one.

'I'm Rachel Berry,' she repeated, cutting short her welcoming speech this time but keeping her voice perky. She was still going to be the best mentor ever, even if this boy seemed less than enthusiastic about her presence.

'Jean-Paul.' Jean-Paul pressed the heel of his hand to his forehead and yawned.

'Yes, I know.' Rachel then noticed that her picture – the photocopy of her yearbook photo that Mr Schuester had given Jean-Paul to identify her – was lying at his feet, half crumpled into a ball. Not only was that rude, but that was littering. 'I, uh, asked Monsieur Renaud for a list of all the students and their matches.' She wanted to make sure everyone else was being an excellent mentor, as well. Some of the Glee kids could be slackers, but she wanted to make sure they did McKinley High proud by repre-senting it well to the French kids.

Jean-Paul made no comment. He fingered his earphone as if he were about to stick it back in his ear.

'Are you still jet-lagged?' Rachel asked politely. She pretended not to see the wad of gum stuck to the outside of her locker. At least it wasn't Jean-Paul's – someone had

76

been sticking a pink wad of chewed gum to her locker every day for the past two weeks.

'No.' Jean-Paul stared somewhere over Rachel's shoulders. His eyes were actually very pretty, and he would have been quite handsome if he knew how to be even remotely polite. But maybe he was just nervous about his poor English skills? That thought made Rachel feel better, and she vowed to do more of the talking so that perhaps Jean-Paul could pick up some English-language tips from her. After all, she had perfect enunciation.

'We have a little time before first period, so I'd love to show you the auditorium where we'll perform at the Multicultural Fair on Saturday night.' Jean-Paul remained silent, which Rachel took as a sign of disinterest. Rachel scrambled for something else. 'Or I could show you our library, which has a passable collection of sheet music, although it has a serious lack of show tunes composed after 1998.'

Nothing. Not even a glimmer of a response from Jean-Paul, whose eyes were glazed over as he stared into the distance.

Rachel was unnerved. While she was used to people trying to ignore her, normally they could only keep it up for so long. Finally, she followed Jean-Paul's eyes to see where they were staring. Across the hall from them, Finn was standing at his locker, deep in conversation with the hot blond girl, Celeste – who Rachel had heard was the alleged star of their group. Finn was wearing a William McKinley High Athletic Department T-shirt and a hooded navy blue sweatshirt that was fading at the cuffs.

She glanced back at Jean-Paul. 'That's Finn Hudson. He's the quarterback of the football team, and also the forward on the McKinley basketball team, and they're undefeated in their division this year.' He also played on the baseball team in spring as the third baseman, but she didn't know how much identifying information she could give about Finn without sounding like a stalker.

'Really?' Jean-Paul asked, straightening slightly. His blue-gray eyes suddenly showed a flicker of interest. 'And he's in your Glee Club?' His English was actually surprisingly good, Rachel thought, for someone who was too shy to talk.

'Yes, he's our star bari-tenor,' Rachel bragged. She, too, brightened visibly. Jean-Paul must just be shy about hanging out with an American girl – maybe he wanted to know more about what the guys did. Well, that was fine with Rachel, as Finn was one of her favorite topics. She was pretty sure she knew more about him than his mother did.

Jean-Paul nodded. 'That is very interesting.'

Rachel beamed. Maybe if she couldn't actually talk *to* Finn, because of her stupid pact with vindictive Quinn Fabray, she could at least talk *about* him.

Finn leaned against his open locker with his backpack slung over his left shoulder. He couldn't believe his luck getting partnered with Celeste. Maybe Mr Schuester thought he owed Finn a favor or something, or maybe he just wanted to keep him happy and make sure he stuck with Glee Club. Finn didn't like to question his good luck. When he walked into school that morning and saw the gorgeous blond girl standing in front of his locker, holding up a picture of him – it was like some kind of dream. She had on a pretty white V-neck sweater, a pair of tight black jeans, and black high heels. McKinley High students stared at the two of them, wondering who the mysterious new girl was and why she was carrying a picture of Finn.

'I'm Celeste,' she'd said, leaning forward to kiss his cheek. Finn was sure his face had flushed as he bent over a little, and she air-kissed one cheek, then the other. She smelled like pears and looked like an exotic, curly haired Quinn – only less familiar and therefore hotter.

And she was way interested in everything he had to say. As he got together his books for first period, she asked all kinds of questions, about McKinley and Ohio and America in general. Her English was great. 'How many students go to McKinley? Where are the big cities in Ohio? Have you ever been to New York?'

Finn answered her questions as best he could – he didn't really know how many students went to McKinley, and he had never been to New York – but he kept finding himself kind of smiling stupidly at her pretty lips and her cute French accent.

'Your English is really good,' Finn spoke up when she stopped asking questions. He slammed his locker door closed. She, in fact, did speak English very well – way better than he spoke Spanish, which he'd been taking since eighth grade. If he were in Spain right now, he'd barely be able to ask where the bathrooms were.

Celeste smiled, her cheeks turning pink. She loved praise. 'Thank you. It is my fourth language. I speak German and Italian as well.'

'Wow.' Finn started to imagine her as some kind of gorgeous, supermodel spy – sort of like Sydney Bristow in *Alias*, a show he'd watch whenever it showed up on cable – when he felt something sharp poking into his shoulder.

He turned round to find a pissed-off-looking Quinn, her arms crossed over the front of her pink turtleneck sweater. Next to her stood a nerdy-looking French boy in dark-framed Artie glasses. 'What am I supposed to do with *this*?' she asked Finn, oblivious to the fact that her French student – and Finn's – could actually understand English. 'I hardly have time to look after myself anymore, let alone some dreary French kid.' *Wow, she seems really stressed out*, Finn thought. *Maybe it's just pregnant girly hormones or something.*

'Be nice,' Finn whispered in Quinn's ear. She wasn't a bad person or anything, but she could be a little snobby and was always treating other people, well, not that nicely.

Finn didn't miss the way she gave him a hard time when he didn't compliment her outfit, or when he talked too slowly, or when he talked to Rachel. It was kind of exhausting. 'I'm Finn,' he said to the French boy to try to cover the awkwardness. He stuck out his hand.

'Nicholas,' the boy answered, shaking Finn's hand. He pronounced his name like 'Nick-o-la', which Finn thought was a little funny. He was grateful Nicholas didn't lean forward to kiss him on the cheeks. Not that he minded with Celeste, but with a dude, it was different.

'Quinn, this is Celeste.' Finn involuntarily took a step backward, as if to get out of Quinn's way. Quinn had a weird proprietary attitude about him that made Finn seriously wonder if she was telling girls behind his back that he had some kind of contagious disease or that they weren't allowed to talk with him. As former head Cheerio, she still had that kind of influence.

Quinn's wide eyes narrowed at the sight of Celeste. Of course Mr Schuester would give the hot girl to his boy Finn – he practically worshipped the ground Finn walked on, probably because Finn was everything he wasn't in high school. And of course he had to torture Quinn by giving her the dorkiest guy. It seemed like Mr Schu was punishing her on some level for that whole weird situation with his ex-wife. It wasn't Quinn's fault that Terri Schuester had totally faked a pregnancy and tried to adopt Quinn's baby as her own. Quinn looked back at her own sad excuse for a partner. Nicholas was actually wearing a *tie* to school. No one wore ties except teachers and Kurt, if he was trying to make a fashion statement.

'Welcome to McKinley High, Celeste.' Quinn's voice was dripping with sweetness. She knew how to turn on the charm, and she didn't want Celeste to know how much she loathed her – at least, not yet. 'How do you like things so far?'

Celeste glanced at Finn, her blue eyes taking him in. 'Everyone seems very nice.' The corners of her lips curved up in a grin.

Quinn put her hands in the back pockets of her uncomfortably snug jeans. She felt Nicholas's beady little eyes checking her out, but she barely bothered to glance at him. All she could think about was how she'd throw herself off a cliff before she let this French trollop spend any more time than necessary alone with Finn. 'Good. I think it would be a lot of fun if the four of us hung out today, don't you, Finn?'

Finn gulped. He glanced at Nicholas, who was clearly not a priority for Quinn right now. She was so distracted, she would probably ditch him in five seconds if Finn didn't do something. He imagined the poor boy wandering the halls of McKinley, getting slushied by jocks who were eager to initiate him. 'Sure,' he said. 'That would be fun.' It was sort of weird how he felt like he was offering to help Quinn babysit.

He glanced at Celeste, who smiled politely at him. Was he imagining it, or did she look a little disappointed? He hoped so. Maybe that meant that he'd get some time later to get to know Celeste a little better, without his ex-girlfriend acting like a chaperone.

eight

Principal Figgins's office, Wednesday morning

When Mr Schuester poked his head in the outer reception area of the principal's office, he was grateful to see that Mrs Goodrich, Principal Figgins's longtime secretary, was not at her desk. She was a sweet woman, but she remembered Will fondly from his days as a high school student, and she would always pinch his cheek and try to give him a cookie from the bag she kept in her bottom drawer. It was nice to walk into Principal Figgins's office unmolested, especially as he was bringing Philippe Renaud with him.

Mr Schuester rapped his knuckles against the open door to Principal Figgins's office. Figgins's leather swivel chair was turned so that he could stare out the plate-glass window at the student parking lot, scanning for telltale puffs of smoke coming up from behind cars as students snuck out for smoke breaks. It was a habit of the principal, even though in the late February weather, it was unlikely he was going to rush out of the school into the icy cold just to catch them in the act. Beneath his desk, his shoes were lined up neatly next to his socked feet. There was a tiny hole near his pinky toe.

'Figgins?' Will asked. He always admired the crisp neatness of the principal's office. The glossy wood desk had little-to-no clutter on it, just a flat-screen computer monitor, a silver framed photograph of Figgins's family turned discreetly toward him, and a pencil holder. Will knew he kept an easily accessible box of tissues in his top drawer for weepy parents. 'Do you have a second to meet a friend of mine?'

Principal Figgins spun around in his chair. 'Of course, Will.' He always sounded tired, even when he didn't seem to be in the middle of any pressing conflict. But high schools were breeding grounds of conflict, and he was always sorting out disputes among teachers over hall-monitor duties or parking spots. It was no wonder he was taking three different pills to control his blood pressure. 'Please come in.'

Will led Monsieur Renaud into the room. 'This is Philippe Renaud, director of the Lycée de Lyon Chorale, and this is our very own Principal Figgins, a staunch supporter of the arts.' He winked at Principal Figgins. Principal Figgins *was* a supporter of the arts – when it didn't cost him too much.

Principal Figgins chuckled and stuck out his hand to shake Philippe's. 'Sucking up is useless, Will. You know I don't have total control over budgets.' His slight Indian accent made everything he said sound pleasant, a quality that came in handy for a principal to have when he was talking to parents about their failing students or to teachers about their classroom cuts. 'I hope you and your students are enjoying your time at our school.'

Monsieur Renaud smiled eagerly. Today he was wearing a pair of dark dress pants, a crisp blue shirt, and a cuffed blazer that Kurt had immediately identified as Armani. ('They must pay teachers much better in France,' he'd whispered to Mercedes earlier that morning, 'because we're never going to see Mr Schuester dressed like *that*.') 'Very much, sir. Everyone has been very kind and welcoming.' That wasn't exactly true, as one of his students – Nicholas – had reported that he'd already been 'slushied', something Philippe didn't fully understand but that seemed to involve a cold beverage being thrown in his face. He suspected it was either some kind of gang initiation or an isolated anti-French incident. He was hesitant to bring it up to the principal, however, as the students seemed to be enjoying their time nonetheless.

'Good. I went to Paris on my honeymoon.' Principal

Figgins smiled fondly, remembering the breakfasts of hot chocolate and croissants. That was back before his wife put him on a strict low-cholesterol diet of egg whites and whole-wheat toast – with no butter. What was the point of toast without butter? 'They have some beautiful women there.'

The outer door to the principal's office slammed shut, and Will groaned at the familiar sound of sneakers pounding angrily across the industrial carpeting of the office. It wasn't the sound itself so much as the fury behind it that was distinctly Sue Sylvester's. No one slammed a door like she did, and no one entered a room with such anger, such self-righteousness. He could recognize those footsteps from his nightmares. A whiff of orange Gatorade hit the air.

One second later, Coach Sylvester appeared in the doorway, the sleeves of her burgundy tracksuit pushed up to her elbows. Her short blond hair was spiked up around her ears, as if she'd just grabbed fists of her own hair in frustration or disgust.

She ignored Will and Philippe and stood directly in front of Figgins's desk. 'Are you aware that the hallways of McKinley have been polluted with the scent of stale cheese, hairy armpits, and cigarettes?'

'Sue!' Principal Figgins got to his feet. The last thing he wanted was Sue Sylvester provoking an incident that would get him on the local news. Sue Sylvester was many things, but culturally sensitive was not one of them, and it made Multicultural Week a stressful time for Principal Figgins. Last year, Sue Sylvester and her Cheerios had boycotted German Day in the cafeteria, sitting outside the lunchroom with posters showing X-ed out old photographs of Hitler youth and headings that read BRATWURST IS ONLY THE BEGINNING, KIDS. Sue claimed her parents were famous Nazi-hunters, but that didn't excuse her insensitive display, especially not to Heidi Gruber, who came to Principal Figgins's office in tears – to which Sue had replied, 'I don't eat bratwurst, Heidi. I get my daily sodium from all the children's tears I cause. So cry me a river.' It had taken Figgins a while to smooth over that one.

'There are a bunch of anti-Americans running amok and mixing with our students. I'm about to call US Immigration Services immediately to get the situation under control.' Sue leaned proprietarily against the bookshelf that housed Principal Figgins's dated Encyclopedia Britannica and stared him down, daring him to challenge her.

'Do you have any idea how offensive you're being?' Will was mortified by her ignorant comments – not that they were that out of line with the other offensive comments that came out of her mouth on a daily basis. But it was humiliating to hear her say them in front of Philippe. What was he going to think of McKinley High now? Hopefully he'd realize that Sue was not a fair representative. 'This is

Philippe Renaud, my good friend and the director of the French glee club. Those kids are his students.'

'Oh, hi, William.' Sue Sylvester turned to him with her fake friendly smile. 'I didn't see you there beneath the magical forest growing on top of your head. I suspect that if I hired a tiny lumberjack to axe those gnarly roots, several fairies would fly out and weep for the loss of their woodland homes.' She hated his hair with something that bordered on fanaticism.

'Calm down, Sue, and show some respect to our foreign visitors. It is, after all, Multicultural Week, and McKinley High could do with a little multiculture.' Principal Figgins sat down again. He felt awkward standing in his socked feet and felt much better when they were hidden under his desk.

'I like the French, Will. I really do.' Sue eyed Philippe with interest. 'I liked them when we rescued them from the Nazis in World War II, and I liked them even more when they gave us Zinedine Zidane, their World Cup soccer player who head-butted an Italian opponent who had said something offensive about his mother in the middle of a championship match.' She thought all professional sports could benefit from a little more aggression.

Philippe blanched visibly as he touched his hand to his stomach. Who was this crazy lady? She couldn't possibly be an educator at this school, not unless the American education system was in total disarray. 'That was a dark moment in French culture. It was very unsportsmanlike.'

Sue's eyes bugged out. 'Unsportsmanlike? He was a hero. If only you French were as fastidious about . . .'

'Thank you, Sue,' Figgins cut her off, not wanting to hear where she was going with that train of thought. He knew it was dangerous to let Sue Sylvester express her opinions in front of newcomers. 'As I was saying, I'm particularly happy to welcome our French visitors, as they are going to perform at the show on Saturday.' He rubbed his hands together to simulate excitement. He would be happy when this whole week was over and things went back to normal. The Mexican food yesterday had kept him bent over a toilet for three hours afterward, and he was still eating Saltines to try to calm his stomach. 'I've secured a special guest to attend the show – the superintendent of the school district, Mr George Doherty.'

'Mr Doherty's going to be at the show?' Will's brain started to spin. He'd hoped that the superintendent would show up at last fall's sectionals to see Glee Club perform, but there had been an emergency at Lima Elementary involving a kindergartner who had overdosed on paste. Maybe this was their chance to impress him.

Figgins nodded wisely and leaned back in his chair. 'Yes. And if he likes what he sees at McKinley, he has promised to channel more district funding into the school's extracurricular activities and academics.'

'That's an amazing opportunity,' Will said, already visualizing the Glee Club number. It would be something classic, something that would appeal to the sixty-year-old Superintendent Doherty, but something with an edge to it as well. Doherty would love it, especially with the presence of the Lycée de Lyon students in the performance as well – it would be the perfect embodiment of Multicultural Week.

'For who? For the *Cabaret*-squealing Glee kids?' Sue reared back in anger, almost knocking over the tiny black globe that sat on Figgins's shelf. Will wondered briefly where she got the energy to be so bitter all the time – the Gatorade? Did all the electrolytes in it somehow increase her bile production?

'Sue, relax. This is a great opportunity for all of the school's extracurricular clubs – not just Glee.' Principal Figgins glanced at the clock on his computer. This day wasn't even close to being over. He had lunch duty today, which meant making sure the kids didn't sit on one another's laps or hurl food at the windows. He just wanted to go home and curl up with some reruns of *House* and a hot cup of tea.

Sue put her hands on Figgins's desk and leaned forward menacingly. 'If that's the case, then I demand my Cheerios have the opportunity to perform as well. If Multicultural Week teaches us nothing else, it should illuminate the fact that overachieving winners deserve the chance to dominate school-run events. I will not tolerate reverse discrimination in this school.' Plus, Sue thought, if the Cheerios received extra funding from Superintendent Doherty, she could certainly find something to spend more money on – their very own tanning booth, perhaps. It was exhausting for her girls to make repeated trips down to Total Tan each week.

Now Will was the one annoyed. Even though the Cheerios had every opportunity on the planet – they performed at every single basketball game! – Coach Sylvester still wanted to horn in on one of Glee Club's rare chances to perform for the student body. 'It's a multicultural show, Sue. What do the Cheerios have to do with culture?'

Principal Figgins sighed. He could see Will's point, of course, but he didn't want Sue Sylvester on his back for yet another reason. He'd learned that it was much easier in the long run to let her have her way. 'Sue, if you can find a way to celebrate culture in your routine, the Cheerios can perform.'

Sue clapped her hands together in triumph. 'We are going to shove cultural tolerance and understanding down Mr Doherty's throat with more vigor than the first time a mama bird regurgitates a worm into the feeble gob of her helpless, malnourished offspring. You watch and you learn, Frog-man.' Those Glee kids were a nuisance, and so were those ripe-smelling, deodorant-fearing Frenchies they'd imported just to annoy her. The Cheerios were going to go ahead and put them right in their place.

nine

McKinley High science wing, between classes,
Wednesday morning

'And tell me again? What is this *Outback Steakhouse*?'
Gerard, Puck's French partner, hurried to keep
up with Puck as they headed down the hallway
toward Puck's biology class. He was short, but he walked
like a tall guy, taking long, confident strides, and Puck
had decided that Gerard wasn't a complete loser. In fact,
a couple of Puck's basketball buddies were walking to class
in front of them, and they kept cracking up at the things
he had to say. He had some kind of weird obsession with
American food and kept asking Puck and the other guys
about the menus at all the chain restaurants he'd seen
on his way from the airport.

'Dude, he doesn't know what Outback Steakhouse is. That totally sucks.' Chris Cole, one of the basketball team's point guards, looked bizarrely crushed by this news.

'I told you. Outback Steakhouse is the awesome one where the MILF waitresses will always slip me a free Bloomin' Onion if I give them the sweet Puckster smile.' Puck and the other guys fist-bumped a football player who had some freshman in a headlock as they passed.

'What's a MILF?' Gerard looked concerned, as if his ten years of English classes had failed him. In his faded jeans and worn-out New York Yankees T-shirt, Gerard looked fairly American, although he wore more gel in his hair than the entire cast of *The Sopranos* combined. 'And a Bloomin' Onion?'

Chris almost snorted blue slushie through his nose. One of the other guys thumped Gerard on the back approvingly. It wasn't often that they got to meet people from different cultures. This kid was kind of like an alien experiment to them – he spoke English well enough, but he didn't know anything important.

'Dude, don't they have *anything* in France?' Puck asked distractedly. 'I didn't think it was supposed to be, like, a Third World country.' Up ahead, Finn was standing by the water fountain, holding his hot blond partner's bag as she leaned over to take a drink. She had on a pair of tight black pants that gave Puck all sorts of bad ideas.

'You've got McDonald's, right?' asked Jared Clark, the

overly tall boy who made the basketball team every year because of his height but who could never score a single basket. 'Is it true that they serve mayo on their French fries?'

'Dude,' Gerard said, picking up on the repeated usage of the word by the jock guys. 'I do not understand this whole "French fry" expression. Why does everyone think they're French?'

Puck interrupted the culinary discussion by punching Gerard in the shoulder. 'What's the deal with that blond chick?' Puck stopped to take a sip from the water fountain so he could keep watching Finn and the blond girl as they walked toward the math wing of the building.

Gerard stopped to wait for him. 'Celeste?' He shrugged indifferently. 'She's nice.'

'Nice?' Puck straightened up and wiped his mouth with the back of his hand. He was disappointed in his partner's inability to dissect the features of a hot girl. 'What about that chick with the short hair? The one who looks like Tinkerbell?'

'Rielle. Yes, she is cool.' Gerard glanced over at a trophy case full of Cheerios awards in order to flex his muscles in the reflection from the glass. 'She plays the guitar.'

Puck rolled his eyes. He didn't care if she was *cool*. Besides, you could tell just by looking at a chick if she was cool or not. He was hoping Gerard would say she liked badass guys with Mohawks who looked like they rode motorcycles, even if they didn't. 'It's totally unfair that I didn't get paired with one of them. I mean, they're being wasted on Finn, who can't seal a deal, and Artie, who's in a wheelchair.' He'd never heard of anyone in a wheelchair getting a chick anyway.

Puck didn't notice that Gerard was starting to walk faster, like he was trying to catch up with the basketball guys. 'I'm still going to try and hook up with one of them, though. Maybe both, if they're lucky.'

Gerard made a funny noise that sounded like a snort. Gerard, who had actually liked Puck and thought he was pretty cool, was a little offended to hear that Puck didn't want him as a partner. And he thought it was strange that Puck seemed abnormally confident about girls.

Puck took the snort personally. 'You don't think I could get one of them? They definitely don't have the Puckster in France, and I'm sure they'd appreciate a taste of something new.' Maybe he'd even invite Rielle to come to the Basketball-Cheerios mixer on Friday night, since Celeste already looked like she was into Finn.

Gerard took a few fast steps forward until he was walking next to Chris and Jared. 'I saw a sign for something called Arby's. What is this?' he asked.

'Man, France sucks!' Chris started explaining the virtues of roast beef sandwiches. Gerard laughed. These guys were pretty amusing – maybe not the sharpest knives in the drawer, but definitely interesting. And if Puck would rather try to hang out with one of the boring girls from Lyon, he could go right ahead and do that. *It's not like they'll ever fall for a stupid American guy*, Gerard thought.

Puck didn't notice Gerard's absence. He was still thinking about the Basketball-Cheerios mixer and that hot Rielle girl, and once he got his mind stuck on a chick, he had to either make out with her, or . . . Puck didn't actually know what would happen if he didn't make out with her – it had never happened before. 'It sucks that you have to sit through bio with me. You want to blow it off?'

He turned to Gerard, but, instead, a perky but socially undesirable freshman girl in a red knit dress was standing next to him, looking hopeful. Farther down the hall, he could see Gerard fist-bumping the basketball guys and laughing uproariously about something. What the hell? Puck did not get ditched – even by a dude.

Puck shook his head at the freshman girl. 'Sorry, not even if I knocked back a few.' He secretly sniffed his armpits as he headed toward the biology door. No, he smelled pretty fresh. Maybe it was too much for these French guys. He had noticed that Gerard smelled a little ripe, like he'd just run a couple of laps.

Before Puck could walk through the door to his biology class, however, he spotted Rielle walking toward him, no Artie in sight. He was probably taking the handicapped elevator. She *did* look like Tinkerbell, with her light brown pixie hair and her big eyes. She had on a short black dress with little puff sleeves and a pair of hot-pink tights, making her look kind of like a pixie rocker. Puck had been with girls fitting all kinds of descriptions, but pixie rocker was new to him.

Leaning against the wall, in classic cool pose, Puck gave her the head nod coupled with the half-smile. It usually left girls tripping over themselves.

But Rielle . . . kept walking.

Puck straightened up before someone else passed and noticed that he'd been dissed. She didn't even notice him? To add to his humiliation, Kurt from Glee – who had actually chosen to wear his turquoise beret out in public – was headed toward him with not one, not two, but *three* French girls hanging on his every word. They weren't the hottest chicks in the world, but they weren't dogs.

'You look so good in the beret,' one of the girls said, her voice dripping with admiration.

'I did not realize American boys would be so stylish,' another girl said.

Kurt tugged the beret lower on his forehead so that it hung at a rakish angle. 'Ladies, the keys to any great style are self-confidence and an excellent taste in accessories.'

What was up with these French kids, damn it? Puck thought. They were all super-weird. What girl could resist Puck? Did his charm somehow not translate into French? If they preferred guys like Kurt, Puck was screwed.

Puck quickly recovered and gave the death stare across the hall to a sophomore, who dropped his books in terror. But it was an unsatisfying victory. He clearly needed to try a little harder – if not for Rielle, then to save his dignity and reputation as the lady-killer of McKinley High. Once it got around that some hot chick – French or not – was immune to his charms, it would be all over for him. There had to be a way for him to get to her.

ten

McKinley High quad, Wednesday lunch

After the resounding failure of Tuesday's Mexican fiesta lunch, the school administration decided to feature a cuisine that was more characteristic of McKinley High's cafeteria food in general – Italian. Instead of importing food from a local Italian restaurant, dining services had decided to rely on some of its old menu stalwarts – greasy cheese pizza, which was served every Wednesday anyway, overcooked spaghetti and spice-less meatballs, and a bland dish that was either eggplant Parmesan or chicken Parmesan. No one was excited about the food, but no one was turned ill by it, either.

By lunchtime Wednesday, it was also clear that, for the most part, the McKinley Glee mentors had been doing a halfway decent job showing their partners around school all morning. The table where the Glee kids sat was crowded with French students, joking with their American counterparts and making fun of the bad food. They had a certain confidence about them – even the normal-looking ones – that made them appear charming and sophisticated. Most of the kids from Lima, Ohio, had never had the chance to meet a French person, and they looked on in awe, occasionally coming up to ask one of the Glee kids to introduce them to their French friends. It was almost like the Glee kids were popular – even if that was temporary.

Best of all, the French kids were interesting. Artie and his partner, Rielle, were having an in-depth conversation about contemporary French cinema, and Angelique, a curvy redheaded girl with black-framed glasses, was drawing an Asterix cartoon on Tina's notebook. Kurt and a collection of French girls were paging through a French *Vogue* that one of them had brought. Only one of them was his partner, but the others had gravitated toward him when their mentors failed to show up that morning at the designated meeting spots. The Cheerios, of course, had been late.

'You eat this food every day?' Mercedes's partner, Marc, asked as he stuck his fork into a dry meatball. He made a funny face. 'Yes?'

'Usually it's worse.' Mercedes giggled. She liked her

partner. Marc was super-fun and bubbly, just like her. As they'd walked through the halls that morning, Mercedes had started to hum the new Usher song. Before she knew it, Marc had started to beat box along with her, and they were giving an impromptu concert in the hallway with everyone staring at them and clapping to the beat. Mercedes wasn't used to being stared at in the good kind of way.

The only problem was that Marc also seemed to be seriously deficient in the style department. His jeans were appallingly blue and so short you could see the white socks he wore with his brown tasseled loafers. His short-sleeved dress shirt featured a blinding orange-and-black plaid pattern. It was such a shame because there was a cute, friendly, talented guy hiding beneath those awful clothes. With some serious fashion consulting, he could be a good-looking guy.

Thankfully, Mercedes considered style an area of exper-tise. She was proud of her entire wardrobe, which was carefully designed to highlight her best assets and hide – or minimize – her worst. That day, she knew she was rocking her off-the-shoulder purple sweater, wide silver belt, and slouchy suede boots. She'd already asked Marc – without telling him why – if he wanted to go check out the mall this afternoon. He was in dire need of a makeover – and not just to fit in with the kids at McKinley. Mercedes didn't care about that. As Kurt liked to say, every moment was an opportunity for fashion. It was simply a shame that Marc was letting all those moments go to waste.

'*Intéressant.*' Marc took a tentative bite of the meatball before putting down his fork. 'I am guessing . . . horse meat?'

Everyone laughed. 'It's a specialty of American cafeteria culture,' Artie said, pushing his glasses back up his nose. 'Only the very best for McKinley High.'

'You know what other part of American culture I really like?' Quinn's partner, Nicholas, said, taking a giant bite out of his piece of garlic bread. He thought his partner was insanely pretty, but she was very cold and did not seem to like him very much. 'California. How far is that from here?'

'Far. There are no California girls here,' Mercedes said, shaking her head. Her long rhinestone earrings shaped like music notes sparkled in the light.

'You know that famous old American song "California Girls"?' Marc asked, and then he put one hand to his mouth and started to beat box. The other hand sort of danced to the rhythm.

Quickly, a small crowd started to gather around. The diva in Mercedes responded to the attention like a flower to sunlight, and she started to sing the lyrics, loud and clear. Aimee, Sophie, and Claire hopped to their feet and came up with some impromptu dance moves and backup vocals. Their tiny corner of the cafeteria – so often ignored by the masses – was suddenly the center of attention.

At the end of the hot food line, Mr Schuester and Monsieur Renaud paused. Mr Schuester packed a brown-bag lunch every morning and ate in the faculty lunch-room, but Philippe wanted to 'get the full student experience' and eat in the cafeteria. His hands clutched a warm tray full of unidentified Italian food. His face, which had paled when the gloved cafeteria lady slopped the food onto his plate with a giant spoon, brightened at the sight of the students jamming together. 'Will, that is priceless.'

'It looks like our plan worked.' Mr Schuester beamed, his dimples in full effect. 'They're even doing musical collaborations outside of class.' He thought back fondly to the days when he was a student and hosted Philippe. Back then, an a cappella trend was still thriving, and he and the other Glee kids would often sing lines to one another when they passed in the hallway. Philippe had fit right in with his deep baritone and his quick sense of humor.

'Not bad, *mon ami*.' By now, Philippe was no longer flustered by the loving gazes directed toward him from giggling American girls. He didn't even notice as the girl in the funny cheerleading outfit brushed past him and dropped a folded napkin with a drawing of a heart on it onto his tray.

But before Mr Schuester could finish patting himself on the back, he spotted Brittany and Santana sitting with a group of Cheerios and basketball players by the window, as they always were. Neither of their French partners was anywhere in sight. 'Hold on a second,' Mr Schuester said to Philippe. He wasn't totally surprised, although he had expected better of his Cheerios this time – he wasn't quite sure why, but he was always giving them the benefit of the doubt. Maybe because they'd spent years under the influence of the soul-sucking Sue Sylvester and had earned some allowances.

He walked over to the girls, who looked up in embarrassment. Not because they'd been caught without their French partners, but because no one wanted to be seen talking to a teacher in the cafeteria. Thankfully, all the other students were distracted as the commotion at the Glee kids' table finally broke up. 'What gives, you guys?' He held his hands out in confusion. 'Why aren't you with Aimee and Sophie?'

Santana sighed heavily, as if deeply burdened by Mr Schuester's presence. She held what looked like a lettuce sandwich in her hand and waved it toward the other Glee kids. 'They're over there.'

The milk sloshed in its container as Mr Schuester set the tray down on the edge of the table. He felt inordinately silly carrying a tray around the cafeteria – he should have just gone ahead and brought his own lunch. 'But you guys are in charge of showing them around!'

Santana shrugged and took a bite of her sandwich. 'We

didn't really want to, so we gave them to Kurt. They seem to like him better, anyway.' Mr Schuester glanced over at Kurt's table. Aimee and Sophie were sitting on either side of Kurt, hanging on to his every word, while another girl, Claire, stroked the lapel of Kurt's jacket. They looked anything but bored, or lost, or abandoned.

Brittany looked up at Mr Schuester with her wide, vacant blue eyes. 'Also, they speak pig Latin, and it's confusing.'

Mr Schuester shook his head. 'Brittany, that's French . . .' he started, but Brittany and Santana had already moved on to a conversation about shoes. He glanced over at their abandoned French partners. Everyone at the table was laughing and smiling as if they'd known one another for years. Maybe it wasn't necessarily a bad thing that the French kids weren't hanging out with the Cheerios. Meanwhile, Kurt flipped lazily through the copy of *Vogue*, his fingers expertly flicking through pages and pages of perfume ads. The French girls at the table watched him, giggling like crazy when he made snarky comments about an outfit or complimented a look. And it was heavenly for him to be around people who appreciated fashion. Maybe he was part French.

'What do you think of the new Versace look?' Aimee asked, blinking her thick dark lashes at Kurt. She was a petite, curvy girl in a khaki green shirt dress with a fabulous red patent-leather belt cinching her waist and a pair of red heels. If Kurt were a woman, he'd wear heels every hour of every day.

'It's fine, if unadventurous.' Kurt adjusted his black bow tie. It was one of his favorite articles of clothing and could always be relied on to add a certain dapper quality to anything. He knew it looked good in contrast with his plaid button-down and slim gray flannel trousers. 'It's nothing like the new spring line from Jean Paul Gaultier.'

All three girls sucked in their breath. 'Yes!' said Claire, a plain-looking girl who still managed to dress like a diva in a pair of skinny navy pants, sky-high wedge heels, and a painted silk tunic. Not everyone was blessed with perfect looks, but it didn't mean you couldn't have an excellent sense of style.

'I have not seen it.' Sophie, an olive-skinned girl in a modlike mustard-yellow turtleneck dress, looked disappointed. Then she leaned forward on her elbows, giving Kurt a seductive smile. 'But tell me about it.'

Kurt's blue eyes lit up. It really *was* like he was in heaven. 'Well, it's equestrian chic meets street punk, outrageous but wearable.' As he started to talk about the distressed khaki jodhpurs with studded leather belts, he was so focused that he failed to note the significance of the dreamy looks in their eyes. He thought they were merely as enthralled by the new line as he was.

Sophie nudged Claire in the ribs. '*Il est parfait,*' she whispered under her breath. 'The perfect boy.' He was cute. He was wise and funny. He knew more about fashion than they did, and he was exceedingly well groomed. The girls had not seen any other American boy with such perfectly clean fingernails, and his hair was sculpted to perfection.

Gaydar was apparently something that got lost in translation.

eleven

McKinley High gymnasium, Wednesday afternoon

I mmediately after last period on Wednesday, the McKinley High gymnasium filled with students eager to get to sports practice and shake out the lingering boredom resulting from an entire day of school. During fall and spring, the green grassy fields were home to all the sports practices, but during the cold Ohio winter, the Albert Radsley Memorial Gymnasium was the hub of athletic activity. The locker rooms were on one side of the gym and led to the school pool. The smell of chlorine and the sounds of the swim team's splashes mingled with the smell of sweat and the squeak of sneakers against the polished hardwood floors of the gym. The girls' and boys' basketball teams alternated practice times on the main basketball court, and the boys were on the court now as a cluster of long-legged girls in shorts lined the bottom bleachers and did homework on their laps as they waited for their turn. On the secondary basketball court, the Cheerios held their practice. Coach Sylvester was presiding at one end with her silver whistle at her lips, still wearing one of her characteristic polyester tracksuits, despite the sweltering heat. As usual, she was yelling at the top of her lungs. 'You think this is hard? Try giving yourself a colonic. That's hard!' The radiators were pumping at full blast.

'This is the McKinley High gymnasium,' Rachel announced to Jean-Paul. She was desperately looking for something to do with him. He'd been completely uninterested in her Rachel Berry highlights tour, and she was exhausted trying to please him. She'd taken him to all the spots around school where important events in her development had occurred – the morning announcements room, which first led to Kurt inviting her to join Glee; the dance studio where Miss Kathy, the dance teacher, called Rachel's plié 'the most extraordinary move' she'd ever seen; exactly where she'd been standing onstage singing 'Tonight' from *West Side Story* when she noticed Finn staring at her. Jean-Paul hadn't been interested in Rachel's life story, but he did show a spark of interest when Finn's name came up.

Encouraged, Rachel suggested they watch basketball

practice, which Jean-Paul immediately agreed to. She'd overheard him that morning talking to Celeste outside the choir room. (It didn't count as eavesdropping if she didn't speak the language, did it?) But Rachel had heard the words *Finn* and *football* – and Jean-Paul did seem to be looking at Finn a lot. Celeste hadn't seemed to want to talk to Jean-Paul, either, probably because he was so broody and distant. He was kind of like a young French Johnny Depp, which made her even more surprised to find out he was interested in sports – why else would he be so interested in Finn? Or maybe he was just one of those guy-guys who only felt comfortable with other males, doing sweaty, male, back-slapping things.

Jean-Paul's long legs quickly climbed the bleachers, and Rachel scurried to follow, holding down her short sweater dress at her sides. 'This is the basketball team?' Jean-Paul asked, somewhat obviously, Rachel thought.

Rachel stared out at the court, fanning herself with the Post-it-laden copy of *Walden* she was reading in English class. (It was never too early to look for essay topics.) 'Yes. They're very good. They won their division two years in a row.'

'Who is the best player on the team?' Jean-Paul glanced up at the banners hanging from the ceiling, most of them advertising the Cheerios' successful runs at the national cheerleading championships. He looked unimpressed.

'Finn,' she replied quickly. He really was the best

player – Rachel wasn't just biased. When she and Finn had dated – briefly – she'd been very eager to attend all his games and learn everything she could about basketball so that she could be a supportive girlfriend. However, her need to know basketball terminology had been cut short when Finn abruptly broke up with her. Still, sitting on the bleachers again made her think of all those glitter-accented posters she'd made with Finn's name on them, and how strong he looked when he was running down the court, taller than all the other guys. Maybe now that her new crush, Jesse, was in the picture, *someone* would be the glad recipient of her unwavering support. But, somehow, imagining herself in a homemade JESSE'S GIRL shirt didn't seem to make her as happy as her TEAM FINN one had. She sighed heavily, trying to erase the icky feeling in the pit of her stomach.

Today, Finn, in a gray T-shirt and long basketball shorts, was standing at the side of the court talking to his French partner, Celeste. He was bouncing the ball on the ground and doing that cute thing where he dribbled it back and forth under one of his legs. Rachel blinked. It was still hard to see Finn with anyone else, no matter how inno-cent. 'That's dribbling,' Rachel blurted out, just to say something. 'It's really just bouncing the ball.'

'Dribbling,' Jean-Paul repeated, leaning forward to watch. He twirled his silver cell phone in his hand. He had strong hands – *he must be a piano player*, Rachel thought. She could imagine his broody face hunched over the piano, morosely pounding on the keys. His dark hair was pulled back into a ponytail again, which was not Rachel's style, but throughout the day, she'd seen several girls do double takes when they saw him.

Rachel frowned as she looked back down on the basketball court. It was nice that Celeste was showing such an interest in her American mentor's daily life, but really – did she need to be standing next to him at basketball practice? It was completely unnecessary. Not that the other boys seemed to mind. In fact, Rachel saw them attempting an inordinate amount of three-pointers, hoping to catch the pretty French girl's eye.

Just ignore them, Rachel thought. She needed to focus on being a better mentor herself, since this was the first time all day Jean-Paul had expressed even a flicker of interest in anything she'd done with him. 'Do you have basketball in France?' Rachel asked politely.

Jean-Paul didn't take his eyes off the court. 'Yes, we have basketball.' Now, Finn, his hair sticking up with sweat, was stretched out on the floor doing push-ups. Celeste, still wearing the dark jeans and top she'd worn at school, leaned against the blue mats that covered the walls, an impressed look on her pretty face. She had on a pair of black high heels that Rachel found inappropriate for high school attire.

'Do you play?' Rachel asked, not able to let go. This

was the most Jean-Paul had spoken since that morning, when he said to her, 'I do not understand this American obsession with television,' when she asked him if France had a version of *American Idol*. But maybe he was just a man of few words.

Some hooting broke out underneath one of the baskets. The short, buff French guy – Puck's partner, Rachel realized – was engaged in some kind of push-up contest with one of the senior basketball players. They were both on the ground, furiously pushing up and down, as the other guys gathered around them, clapping their hands and cheering in support. It looked like Gerard was winning, despite the fact that he was still wearing his school clothes while the other boy was in his practice outfit. Under the other basket, Puck was practicing layups with some other guys from the basketball team and glanced over his shoulder at his partner.

'I play football,' Jean-Paul said suddenly. 'But what you Americans call *soccer*, not the American football game.'

Okaaaay. Rachel tapped her fingers against her knees. Everything Jean-Paul said came out cranky and bitter. It was like he hated her for some reason, and he didn't even know her! He could maybe be cute, if he cut his hair and got a better attitude.

'I played soccer one year. In first grade. My dads – I have two of them – thought it might help give me a competitive edge in my dance classes.' Rachel couldn't

114

imagine parents more supportive than her own, even though the soccer experiment had been a disaster. 'But I got a soccer ball kicked right at my solar plexus – it had come dangerously close to hitting my larynx and ruining my singing career forever.'

Jean-Paul turned his blue-gray eyes on Rachel. He didn't say a single word.

So much for bonding over soccer. Rachel glanced back at Finn. She'd never had to work hard to have a conversation with him. Everything just came so . . . easily.

But she did not like what she was seeing now. Finn had rolled onto his side, pretending to collapse from exertion. Celeste, giggling, mock-kicked him in the stomach with her high heels, and a moment later, she was on the ground, trying to do a push-up herself. Finn coached her, leaning down close to her head, as she balanced on her arms and the pointy toes of her shoes for a second before collapsing in a heap. Laughing, Finn stretched down his hand and pulled her to her feet.

The scene did not escape the eagle eyes of Quinn, who was perched high up in the back row of the gym. She had planned to take a nap on the bleachers during practice while Finn entertained their two foreign wards. As exhausted as she was, Quinn failed to drift off at all, thanks to the combination of the hard bench, the squeaking of sneakers on hardwood, and the all-too-familiar loud tirades against leg quivers from Coach

Sylvester. So, in an attempt to avoid any conversation with Nicholas, who sat awkwardly watching practice on a lower bench, she pretended to study her Spanish textbook. That is, until she spotted the major flirting session taking place down on the court.

Regardless of what she was doing or whom she was with, Quinn was always acutely aware of what Finn was doing every time he was in the same room. Usually, he wasn't doing anything – he was fairly boring – but it killed Quinn to think of him having more fun with another girl than he'd had with her. That's why she'd been so obsessed about keeping him away from Rachel. For some reason, they seemed to have some kind of deeper connection than Quinn had ever had with him, and it pissed her off.

Now, however, this curly haired French harlot seemed more of an immediate threat. After all, Rachel wasn't even allowed to talk to Finn right now – if only Quinn could keep the agreement alive until they graduated, Rachel would be taken care of.

Celeste was something different entirely. She was much prettier than Rachel, to begin with, and she didn't dress like a thrift-store toddler. Quinn's eyes narrowed as Celeste started inexpertly bouncing the basketball, and Finn guarded her, pretending she was a dangerous player. They both were laughing like idiots. Nearby, Santana stood strong atop the pyramid – Quinn's old spot. The half twist she dropped into on her way down into a perfect basket catch aptly mirrored what Quinn's insides felt like after seeing both Celeste and Santana slide effortlessly into her old roles as flirty tease and head Cheerio.

'Santana.' Coach Sylvester blew into her whistle. 'That fierce look in your eye reminds me of a young Sue Sylvester, back when I competed in the giant slalom at the Calgary Olympics despite my raging hepatitis outbreak. But don't get too cocky. The only way to impress Sue Sylvester is to *be* Sue Sylvester.'

On the bleachers, Rachel and Jean-Paul sat in awkward silence. Jean-Paul just seemed bored, but Rachel was stewing. This was *not* going to do. Rachel, with her enthusiasm and bubbly personality, deserved to have the best French partner, not the worst. Getting Jean-Paul to speak was like pulling teeth – he clearly just did not appreciate her personality. And she had so much to give! She couldn't put up with this any longer – she was going to have to talk to Mr Schuester about it when they got to Glee practice.

All of a sudden, Jean-Paul got to his feet and crossed his arms over his chest. 'Can we go now?' he asked angrily as he stuffed his cell phone into his back pocket.

Rachel blinked. Was he actually crazy as well as moody and rude? She got to her feet. 'Yes, of course.' Rachel slowly followed him down the steps, careful not to let her penny loafers slip on the polished wood bleachers.

As she climbed down, she couldn't help watching Finn

117

as he showed Celeste how to shoot the ball. Once, Finn had taken her bowling, and he'd been an excellent teacher, showing her how to hold the ball and how to line it up with the arrows so that she might actually hit a few of the pins.

Rachel felt she had to face the facts: he'd moved on. He was teaching someone else, and there was nothing Rachel could do about it. All the guys had stopped their drills and were watching, with interest, as Finn stood right next to the girl, his arms touching hers as he showed her how to arc the ball into the air. *Ugh.*

Maybe the gym was a bad choice of a hangout venue after all. Rachel followed her French partner toward the door to the gym, feeling nearly as grumpy as Jean-Paul was acting.

Maybe Multicultural Week was not all that it was cracked up to be.

twelve

Art room and hallway, Wednesday after school

The McKinley High art room was located on the first floor of the original school building, and while it hadn't been the beneficiary of renovations in years – unlike Sue Sylvester's pet projects, the weight room and the exercise studio – it still had its charms. Enormous windows lined the walls, and the floor was the same polished hardwood that was found in the gymnasium, except here they were paint-splattered. Three walls were covered with student work completed with varying degrees of success. The fourth wall was lined with metal shelves where students stored their art supplies and their works in progress. A giant kiln sat in the corner, surrounded by sad-looking pottery projects, many chipped and misshapen.

A few students were scattered around the room, finishing up painting or drawing projects to be hung on the walls for the Multicultural Show. It was one of the rare spots in the school where the radiators didn't function, so, during winter, it felt like a meat locker. Ms Kowalski, the art teacher, who was going through menopause, insisted that the cold helped the creative juices flow, although everyone knew that she just liked the relief from her hot flashes.

The wooden tabletops could be raised to form easels, and Tina and her French partner, Angelique, were sitting at adjacent tables, both wearing their winter coats. Tina had her easel raised and was working on a hyperrealistic oil painting of a Chinese lotus blossom, while Angelique was drawing in Tina's sketchbook with colored pencils.

'That's actually really good.' Tina looked over at Angelique's drawing. It was a sketch of some kind of outdoor farmers' market in a city, the old stone buildings in the background complemented by stalls of brightly colored fruits and vegetables. 'Are you drawing from memory?'

Angelique smiled weakly and pushed a lock of curly brown hair out of her eyes. 'Yes. There is a market by my house. In Lyon.' Perhaps Mr Schuester and Monsieur Renaud had thought it would be a good idea to pair the two shyest students together, but the plan didn't seem to be working that well. Tina had shown Angelique round school all day, but Angelique didn't speak English that well, and because Tina wasn't the most talkative person herself, there were a lot of long moments of silence between them. Tina wished she could be a better host – earlier in the hallway she'd passed Rachel, who was like a tour guide on crack, pointing out every tiny tidbit of information about McKinley High, its students, and America in general. Even though the tall, moody boy looked unimpressed, Tina wished she had a little of Rachel's confidence.

But at least she hadn't ditched her partner, like some people. The Cheerios had completely given up on the whole partnering project. Tina had spotted Puck's short, stocky partner hanging out in the cafeteria, Puck-less, with a group of Neanderthal basketball players having a contest to see who could chug the most red slushies without getting brain freeze.

'I bet Ms Kowalski would let you hang it in the show on Saturday,' Tina offered. On Friday after school, the art students would be hanging up their work in McKinley's main hallways to showcase their talent for the families and visiting schools who would attend the Multicultural Fair the next day. Angelique's quick drawing was better than a lot of the other things that would be hanging on the walls. McKinley High's art department was almost as poorly funded as its music department.

Angelique's face turned pink. She was cute, but in a

quiet way that never would have attracted the attention of someone like Puck. She wore a plain-looking brown scarf wrapped around her neck, and her hair was a color that could only be described as mousy brown. '*C'est possible*,' she said slowly, setting down her pencils to rub her numb fingers.

Tina sighed and turned back to her own painting. She was wearing a pair of cotton gloves without fingertips that she kept in her locker especially for art class use – she still had flexibility with her drawing and painting utensils, yet her fingers didn't feel like they were going to drop off. She'd offered them to Angelique, who had refused. She was failing as a mentor, she could tell. But she just had too many other things to focus on right now. She had the Glee number for the show to worry about – they hadn't heard the French glee kids sing yet, and what if they were all better than the Americans, and Mr Schuester demoted Tina to shaking a tambourine or swaying in the background?

Also, Tina was an active member of the Asian Student Union. She'd been chosen to be the dragon's head in the traditional Chinese dragon dance to celebrate the recent Chinese New Year. It was a big honor, and it took a lot of practice to get it right – she basically had to lead the whole procession around the stage and up and down the aisles of the auditorium. The only reason she was remotely *not* terrified about the whole thing was because her face would be covered by the dragon's head, and no one in the audience would really know who she was. But what if she tripped and fell on her dragon face? She never should have agreed to it.

A familiar noise from the hallway reached Tina's ears – it was the sound of Artie's wheelchair, whose one wheel squeaked when it was cold out. She stopped painting for a moment, holding her brush midair, hoping Artie was coming to see her. He knew he could find her in the art room most afternoons, and the thought of him looking for her brought a smile to her face.

But she caught only a glimpse of Artie, who was deep in conversation with his French partner, Rielle. He didn't stop by the art room door, or even glance in.

'Artie!' Tina called out. She was eager for anyone to break the awkward silence in the room. Maybe Artie and his partner could stop and talk to Angelique for a while.

Seconds later, Artie had wheeled back to the doorway. His pretty partner peeked in at the art room curiously. 'Oh, hi, Tina.' He and Rielle were in the middle of a conversation – in French – about the influence of Bob Dylan on French folk music. Artie thought that Rielle was fascinating to talk to, and even though his French was far from perfect, they were having a pretty deep conversation.

'Hi.' Tina wiped the back of her hand against her nose, worried she had a paint smudge. Why was Artie unenthusiastic about talking to her? Maybe he was just so committed to being a good mentor that he didn't want to be distracted by talking to anyone else.

Rielle said something in French to Angelique, and the two girls and Artie burst into laughter. Only Tina stood there, missing the joke, and hoping it wasn't at her expense.

'I guess we'll see you at practice,' Tina said. Usually she didn't feel nervous around Artie, but something about him seemed different. She didn't even know he spoke French so well.

'Most definitely.' Artie halfheartedly raised his hand in a wave before he and Rielle continued down the hallway.

Angelique looked at Tina with curiosity. She blew on her fingers to warm them up. 'Is Artie your boyfriend?'

Tina almost dropped her brush. Instead, she set it carefully down on the plastic palette next to her easel. 'Artie? No . . . we're, um, just friends.'

Angelique watched Tina's face carefully. She put down her colored pencils. 'That is interesting.'

Tina's face flushed. Across the room, two seniors were putting the finishing touches on a to-scale model of the Taj Mahal, made completely out of toilet paper tubes and sculpted cotton balls. She hoped they were out of earshot. 'Why do you say that?'

Angelique smiled. Her eyes were a very pretty shade of green, almost like the shade of cobalt Tina was using in the lotus leaf. 'I do not know. Your face?'

Tina adjusted the black scarf holding her hair back. She suddenly felt warm, and she unzipped the front of her black puffy coat. Tina hadn't really talked to her friends about Artie, mostly because Kurt and Mercedes, her closest friends, were friends with him, too, and she didn't want anything to be awkward. Maybe Angelique was the perfect person to discuss relationship stuff with – she didn't really know Artie, and she was leaving the country soon, anyway. Besides, it would give them something to talk about.

'We went out a couple of times,' Tina finally admitted. She stared out the window at two girls building a snowman on the school's front lawn. They actually had all the snowman accessories – sticks for arms, a carrot for the nose, a pipe for its mouth. 'But then, I don't know. Nothing else ever happened.'

Angelique nodded slowly. Her curly brown hair had a slight frizz problem, and her nose seemed to be running, possibly because of the oil-paint fumes lingering in the air. Even so, she suddenly seemed wise. 'Do you like him? Still?' she asked.

Tina picked up her brush. She hadn't really thought about it in such black-and-white terms. It all had seemed so complicated in her head, but now, it did seem to come down to Angelique's simple question. Tina didn't really have to think about her answer. 'Yes,' she replied.

Meanwhile, as Artie and Rielle headed down the nearly empty hallways to the choir room, Artie was decidedly not thinking about Tina. He was having too awesome a time with his partner. It wasn't just because she was hot – which she was, with her choppy brown hair and the cute black dress she was wearing that dipped down in the back and showed off her elegant shoulder blades. But she was also smart and funny, even in her limited English, and she loved to hear Artie speak French. It turned out that Rielle was actually a very talented musician who had written a dozen or so songs of her own. 'Do you want to listen to one?' she had asked him shyly as she fiddled with her iPod. 'I recorded a few . . . tracks? But I am not finished with them yet.'

'I would love to hear them,' Artie said, stopping his wheelchair. He took Rielle's earphones and gently placed them in his ears. It seemed like a strangely intimate trans-action. Rielle spun through the songs and clicked on one. Her voice, accompanied by her acoustic guitar, immedi-ately washed over him. It was amazing, kind of folk-rock with an edge.

He had forgotten all about Tina.

The two of them arrived at the choir room before anyone else had gotten there. He was grateful for a few more minutes alone with her.

'We are early,' Rielle said, running her hands gently over the piano keys. She started to hum one of the melo-dies she'd written that Artie recognized from her iPod.

'I can play the guitar, if you want to try out one of

your songs.' Artie knew that girls liked guitar players, but the wheelchair probably negated any guitar points scored. He didn't even know why he bothered hoping for more than just friendship with Rielle – he was just like Cyrano de Bergerac with his huge, obstructive nose, but in Artie's case, it was his huge, awkward wheelchair. Something a nose job couldn't cure. But he knew it wasn't just that, either. Artie was a nice guy, and nice guys didn't get the girls. Girls, for some unknown reason, gravitated toward jackasses like Puck.

Rielle's wide brown eyes lit up at the mention of the guitar. She had tiny pink butterfly barrettes in her hair that seemed ironic instead of cutesy. 'You play? Yes, I would like for you to . . .' she paused.

'Accompany you?' Artie suggested. He rolled over to where an acoustic guitar sat on a stand near the piano. He slung the strap over his shoulder and strummed a few strings. There was something soothing about the weight of a guitar in his hands. It made him feel like a real musician.

A smile crossed Rielle's face. 'Yes, that is the word.' She adjusted a butterfly barrette. 'Maybe . . . also you can help me find English words? For the, uh . . .' she trailed off, searching for the term. 'The words that go with the music?'

'Lyrics.' Artie smiled. Her English was totally adorable. Everything about her was. Maybe in a perfect world, he'd have the nerve to ask her out, but there was no way this hot, talented French girl would be interested in Artie as anything more than a friend. He had *friend* written all over his forehead.

Maybe that just had to be the way. He'd finished the *Cyrano* play last night, and the ugly but brilliant guy did not get the beautiful girl.

'Lyrics!' Rielle thumped the heel of her hand against her forehead, as if she were stupid for not knowing the word. 'You will help?'

'Of course I'll help.' Artie reached around to the back of his wheelchair to where his backpack was hanging – one advantage to being in a chair – and pulled out his notebook.

'You are the best,' Rielle said, beaming at Artie, although the words came out like 'You are zee best' as if she were in a James Bond movie.

Friends, Artie thought as Rielle started to hum the music to a song, her tiny pink lips pursed together delicately. You could never have enough of them.

thirteen

Locker room, Wednesday after basketball practice

Finn was one of the last guys to hit the showers after basketball practice. He was having too good a time hanging out with Celeste to realize how late it was getting, and it wasn't until half the team came out of the locker room smelling of shampoo and deodorant that he realized he needed to hurry up and shower before Glee practice. He gave Celeste directions to the choir room and told her he'd meet her there.

It was nice to have the locker room almost to himself so he could belt out some tunes in the shower without any of the other guys throwing jockstraps at him or making fart noises. As he sang his favorite REO Speedwagon song and soaped up, he couldn't stop thinking about

Celeste. She was really awesome – she had that certain *je ne sais quoi* that people like Kurt were always talking about, although he wasn't quite sure what it meant. And she was totally different from the confusing, high-strung American girls, like Quinn and Rachel. When they were dating, Quinn was always telling him what to do, what to wear, and whom to talk to, which was some nerve for a girl who had been hooking up with his best friend behind his back. And after he'd been dating Rachel for less than a week, she had a relationship calendar printed up so that they'd never forget the anniversary of all their firsts: the first time Finn talked to her, the first time Finn told her she had an amazing voice, the first time Finn kissed her. Then *she'd* broken up with *him*. Crazy, right? He'd bet that she had probably penciled in 'First Breakup' afterward, too. Rachel was a fan of details.

But thinking about Rachel made him feel a little weird, so he turned his mind back to Celeste as the hot water beat down on his shoulders. She had a beautiful voice – sexy, raspy, and with a strong French accent that made him think of the classified ads in the back of the *Playboy*s that were always circulating in the locker room – and that hair. She was like Goldilocks, and Finn thought maybe – just maybe – she might be kind of interested in him. She touched his arm or his back every chance she got, which might have just been a French thing along the lines of cheek kissing.

Finn had spaced out so long he realized he didn't hear the sounds of the other guys anymore and must be the last one out of the locker room. He quickly grabbed his oversized white towel from the hook near the shower door, rubbed his hair dry, and wrapped the towel around his waist. He padded back to his locker in his flip-flops, which squished against the concrete floor. He'd been so busy daydreaming about Celeste that he almost wasn't surprised to get to his locker and hear a familiar French voice come from behind him.

'I like your towel, Finn.'

Finn spun around. Celeste, her long legs crossed daintily at the knee, was perched on one of the benches in the middle of the room, watching Finn with a cute smirk on her face. Her delicate white sweater made her look angelic, although the smile on her face was anything but.

Finn blinked his eyes, but she didn't disappear. Celeste was still sitting there, completely out of place in front of the red lockers where guys kept their jockstraps.

He felt like he was in *Varsity Blues*, one of the most awesome sports movies of all time. This could not be happening, could it?

'It looks good on you,' Celeste said, looking at Finn's abs. He was suddenly grateful he'd been doing two hundred sit-ups every night in his room. The way Celeste's pink lips formed words slowly in English, as if they were still learning the ropes, was supercute.

Finn's face felt like it was on fire. He glanced down as he tightened his towel. He wished he had on some real clothes – or that Celeste was talking to him somewhere other than the locker room, which smelled perpetually of sweat and – Finn hated to think this, with such a delicate girl right in front of him – farts.

'Wha . . . what are you doing? I mean, how did you get in here?' Finn felt like it was he who couldn't speak English. He leaned back against his locker, trying to act casual.

Celeste smiled and got to her feet. The rest of the locker room was silent as her heels clicked against the floor and she made her way over to him. 'I think it is called . . . a door.' She traced a fingernail – long but unpolished – along his bare bicep, bringing goose bumps to his skin.

Finn stupidly stared down at the arm Celeste had touched. 'No, I mean . . . what are you *doing* . . .'

Before he could finish his question, Celeste leaned forward. Her huge blue eyes locked on to his, and they had a confidence in them that was so attractive. As if she'd been waiting all day for this moment, she placed her lips against his and kissed him.

Finn had one second of hesitation – he was still wearing just a towel, after all. What if it fell off? – before he started kissing her back. This was crazy – exactly the kind of thing you read about in the letters to the editor in one of the old *Playboy*s. Her mouth tasted sweet and fruity, reminding Finn of the time he had gelato at the gelato booth at the Galleria Mall. Was gelato French?

Then she twisted her hands in Finn's damp hair, and he forgot about being nervous or worrying about how funky the locker room smelled. If Celeste was a fair representation, French girls were awesome kissers – and maybe *they* were the forward ones, not the American girls. Finn had never had to work so little in his life.

'Oh, Finn,' Celeste murmured as she nibbled on his ear.

Ooh la la, Finn couldn't help thinking. He stepped back from Celeste for a second – everything was moving so fast, and he wanted to stop and enjoy it more. As it was, he had to keep thinking about the time he'd been driving with his mother right after he'd gotten his learner's permit and he'd hit a mailman crossing the street. The memory of the postal worker's body crashing into his windshield was the only thing that could keep Finn from getting too excited. It was difficult, though, when Celeste kept on kissing him, her soft lips moving down his neck.

He rubbed his hand along her back. Her sweater felt soft under his fingertips. 'I'm really happy that you like me. I mean, I couldn't really tell before, if you were just being nice or whatever. But I really like you, too,' he confessed. He wondered how much it would cost to buy a plane ticket to France. Probably more than what he had stuffed in his Vince Lombardi piggy bank. Still, Celeste was proof that French kisses must have originated in France. It would be worth anything to see her again.

Celeste stopped kissing Finn's neck and took a step backward. There was a funny look on her face, and Finn was suddenly sorry he'd interrupted their make-out session to talk. Maybe that's not how the French did it. Finn opened his mouth to say something else.

'Oh no,' Celeste said, glancing at her watch. Her voice sounded unnaturally high. 'We will be late for rehearsal. You must get dressed. I will see you there.'

With that, Celeste spun on her heel and quickly left the room, leaving Finn standing there in his towel. *What just happened?* He rubbed a hand across his face but couldn't keep the smile off it. He couldn't figure out American girls – how was he supposed to understand French ones? Maybe girls all over the world were equally complicated and mind-boggling.

Still, Celeste's abrupt exit couldn't dampen the giddiness he felt at her completely unexpected advances. He whistled to himself as he patted down his body and stepped into his clothes.

He'd never had so much fun in the locker room in his life.

fourteen

Choir room, Wednesday afternoon

The choir room was crowded with people on Wednesday afternoon – all of the McKinley High Glee members were there, with the exception of Finn, as well as the Lycée de Lyon kids. The partnering experiment seemed to have mixed results. Quinn and the Cheerios sat by themselves in plastic chairs on the top tier of the room, leaning against the wall and texting one another snide comments about the hygiene of their European guests. In the front row, Aimee, Sophie, and Claire were clustered around Kurt as he detailed plans to redecorate his basement bedroom in French harem chic.

'You know so much about room design,' Aimee murmured. 'You could be *un décorateur d'intérieur.*'

'I do watch a lot of HGTV.' Kurt leaned back in his chair and smoothed down his plaid shirt. 'I'm a firm believer that feng shui does not mean you can't still be fashionable. I hope to have my own TV show one day.'

The girls nodded slowly, not understanding all the words Kurt was using but appreciating his wisdom nonetheless.

Kurt nodded toward Aimee's red belt. 'That belt is fabulous, by the way.' Aimee blushed furiously.

Artie was strumming the guitar while Tina, Mercedes, Rielle, and Celeste sang the old Beatles song 'Michelle', which included a chorus in French that everyone could sing. Rielle and Celeste taught the other girls how to pronounce the French lines, and Mercedes's partner, Marc, contributed some beat boxing to make the whole thing sound hipper.

Puck sat alone at the drum set, pounding on the drums in a way that accentuated his biceps in an effort to catch Rielle's eye, to no avail. She was too busy with her little sing-along with Artie and the other nerds. *Can't French people identify American losers? A hot girl like Rielle should be hanging with hot guys, like me,* he thought.

Puck hadn't seen Gerard after he'd ditched him to hang out with the other basketball guys, but he seemed to be doing fine on his own now. Mike Chang and Gerard, who turned out to be surprisingly agile, were break-dancing in the middle of the floor. Still, Gerard couldn't stop talking about food. 'You've never had a *croque monsieur*? Are you an alien?' he asked as he executed a perfect cross-legged flare.

Rachel had been sitting off to the side, pretending to look at her homework as everyone else in the room seemed to be having fun. All the French kids were talking and laughing, except for hers. Jean-Paul had claimed to be interested in the shelves of sheet music that lined the front wall of the room just to avoid having to talk to her for one more minute. What was his *deal*? Could he not handle talented women?

Mr Schuester and Monsieur Renaud leaned back against the piano, watching the scene, as they relived the greatest moments of Philippe's own stay at McKinley years earlier. They hadn't had cell phones then, and e-mail was pretty much nonexistent, but music had still been something that could bring all kinds of different people together.

Finally, Finn stumbled through the door, his backpack still half open and his practice clothes sticking out of it. The collar of his striped polo shirt was popped up, like he'd thrown it on in a rush. 'Sorry,' he mumbled as Mr Schuester glanced at his late entrance. 'Practice, uh, ran a little late.'

He had a goofy look on his face that immediately aroused the suspicions of Quinn and Rachel. Why did he look so happy? They watched, with jealous interest, as he collapsed into the chair next to Celeste, although they also both noted, with even more interest, that Celeste gave him just a faint smile before turning back to Mercedes and the others, who had just finished singing.

'Hey,' Finn whispered to Celeste as he tapped her on the shoulder.

Celeste glanced back at him. 'Yes?' she asked, as if he'd interrupted something.

'Oh, sorry.' But Finn couldn't help smiling. Just ten minutes ago, she'd been sucking on his earlobe, and now they were sitting here in the choir room together. He wanted to talk to her about it, but maybe now wasn't the time. 'I just . . .'

Mr Schuester clapped his hands together loudly, calling everyone to attention. Finn reluctantly settled back in his chair. They'd have to wait to talk about their steamy make-out session – or better, to repeat it – until later.

'I hope everyone had a great day getting to know one another. I'm really excited to begin work on our song this afternoon for the Multicultural Fair. But first, because we got our chance yesterday to perform for our French guests, it's their chance to perform for us.' Mr Schuester smiled, his dimples dancing on his face. 'Drumroll, please!' he called out to Puck. 'Lycée de Lyon students, show us what you've got.'

The French kids quickly gathered around the piano, whispering things in French to one another as the McKinley kids hooted and clapped enthusiastically. Puck vacated the drum stool while Marc, in his tragically bright orange plaid shirt, took his seat and expertly spun the sticks around in his fingers. Celeste stepped out in front, adding a few last-minute instructions, and Rachel's heart sank. Celeste was their vocal and spiritual leader, just like Rachel was for the McKinley High group. It was bad enough that Rachel had to spend an entire day with a partner who thought she was as interesting as steamed spinach, but everything would be ten times worse if Celeste turned out to be a better singer than she was.

Celeste smiled graciously at her audience. Rachel pressed her lips tightly together and crossed her legs at the knee. 'This is a song called *"Ce Jeu"* by the French pop star Yelle.' Rachel thought she detected professional vocal training in Celeste's voice. Why hadn't she noticed before?

Kurt nodded, impressed. He tapped the toe of his Bruno Magli wing tips against the floor. 'This song is totally hot,' he whispered to Tina. He loved listening to Euro pop on his satellite radio and knew all the hottest songs. They were easier to dance to than American pop.

Marc counted in French – '*un, deux, trois, quatre*' – as he tapped the drumsticks against the drums before everyone burst into song. It was a catchy tune with a fast beat, and even though no one from McKinley could understand all the lyrics, it was obvious that the Lycée de Lyon Chorale was good.

Especially Celeste. Rachel's worst fears were confirmed once Celeste strode to the front of the room, singing the lead vocals with confidence. She was a strong soprano – and she sounded amazing. She moved with confidence, weaving back and forth among the other students as she sang her solos. Other students stepped in here and there, and they all sounded great, but it was clear that Celeste was their star. Her face glowed with enthusiasm.

She was their Rachel Berry.

Rachel felt her fingers start to tremble with jealousy. She sat on them to keep them still. It was not fair that Celeste could sing like this – she got to be thin and blond and stunning, and Finn, the only boy Rachel had ever really cared about, was staring at her with his mouth open slightly. She could practically see the drool oozing out.

It was true – Finn was thunderstruck by Celeste's talent. He had thought he'd been crazy about Celeste before, but once she started singing, it was an entirely different game. He was a sucker for real musical talent – he still could remember, when he wanted to, how it felt the first time he heard Rachel singing in the auditorium. This wasn't quite the same thing, but it was close.

'Isn't she awesome?' Finn whispered to Kurt, who was sitting next to him. He was wearing a bow tie, which Finn thought was weird. On the other side of Kurt, Rachel's ears perked up. *What is so important that Finn can't wait until after the performance?* She leaned closer to eavesdrop.

Finn was sitting so close to him, all Kurt had to do was inhale slightly and a soapy-clean scent stung his nose. Kurt tried to concentrate on Celeste, who was pretty sensational. He even approved of her sense of style. 'She reminds me of a young Vanessa Paradis.'

Finn's brown eyes blinked. He was busy staring at Celeste. 'Who?'

Kurt sighed heavily, turning his eyes to Finn. He was beautiful but clueless. 'The most famous French pop singer of the last two decades and baby-momma and soul mate to style icon Johnny Depp.' Kurt normally didn't approve of the scruffy look, but Johnny Depp could really do no wrong.

'Oh.' Finn turned back to Celeste, who was flinging her hair as she belted out the last verse. *Unnecessary*, Rachel thought. Vocal talent should stand on its own. 'She did say she was in a big show in Paris when she was younger,' Finn whispered back to Kurt.

Rachel had heard every word of their conversation, and she was about to lose it. Celeste had been in a big show? Rachel knew she wasn't supposed to talk to Finn – Quinn was here, after all, but she didn't care. She *had* to know more about this Celeste girl. How dare she be so talented!

She leaned forward past Kurt and tapped Finn on the arm. 'What show?' she whispered, trying to sound as if she were merely curious, instead of crippled with jealousy.

Finn's face scrunched up as he tried to remember. Rachel found herself trying very hard not to roll her eyes. Why could Finn never retain vital information in that brain of his? Was it too crammed with sports statistics and video game secrets to have any space left over for the things that really mattered? 'Les . . . Les Miser-something?' he finally said.

Rachel almost fell off her chair. Celeste had been in a run of *Les Misérables*? In Paris? Rachel's favorite show – or second favorite, depending on her mood – of all time? On what was probably the French equivalent of Broadway, if there even was a French equivalent of Broadway. Even if Celeste had just played one of the street urchins, it was totally unfair.

Despite all the opportunities she'd had in life – extensive vocal training since she was three months old; advanced jazz, ballet, and tap dance lessons; her own personal psychotherapist to listen to all her deepest hopes and dreams – Rachel had never been in a major production of . . . anything.

Watching Celeste sing, Rachel was forced to admit that she'd met someone every bit as talented as she was. She'd hoped that wouldn't happen until she performed at nationals, or she went on to Juilliard or some university with a world-class music department – but the day had come today, and it didn't feel good.

Rachel quickly recovered, at least on the surface, and

clapped politely along with the more enthusiastic clapping of the rest of Glee Club. Loudest of all was Finn, who actually put his fingers in his mouth and did one of those piercing whistles that only guys seemed to know how to do.

But inside, Rachel was still seething. She could *not* have some random girl from France roll into McKinley High and completely upstage her. Rachel was the best thing that had happened to the music department since the invention of the piano, not Celeste Whatever Her Name Was. Celeste was talented, all right, but she didn't have Rachel's determination and tenacity.

After the performance, the Glee kids got up and started to mingle with the French students, congratulating them and asking all kinds of questions. Brittany managed to casually lean against the piano next to Monsieur Renaud. 'So, do you ever have fantasies involving, like, American things? Like cheerleaders?' she asked, batting her eyelashes at him.

Finn made a beeline for Celeste, who was talking to Mr Schuester. The look on Mr Schuester's face confirmed Rachel's worst fears – that he was just as amazed with Celeste's talent as Rachel was. If Celeste got a bigger role in the dual performance the groups were doing on Saturday, Rachel was going to go into cardiac arrest. She could take only so much bad news in one day.

And as long as she was at it, it wasn't fair that Celeste

was getting Finn, either – not when Rachel couldn't even talk to him. It was just insulting. It was obvious to Rachel that the only way she could retain her dignity in this world was by making it clear to Celeste that both Finn and McKinley High were Rachel Berry's turf and that there wasn't room for two ingenues here.

Mr Schuester stepped into the center of the room, still applauding like crazy. 'I think we can all agree that the Lycée de Lyon Chorale is incredible, and I can't wait to hear how you guys sing together.'

Rachel sighed dramatically. If she didn't sing lead, she was going to pack up her things and storm right out of there. But . . . what if Mr Schuester actually *wanted* her to leave, so that Celeste could shine in the spotlight all by herself? Rachel decided to stay.

And fight, if she had to.

Mr Schuester grabbed a sheaf of papers from his leather messenger bag. 'Monsieur Renaud and I decided to try a mash-up of "Love Train" by the O'Jays and an upbeat version of the classic "L'Hymne à L'Amour" by one of the greatest French singers of all time, Edith Piaf.'

'In French?' Puck asked, his expression skeptical. 'I just mastered English.' He tried to wink at Rielle, but she was talking to Artie. God, if Artie got a girl over him, Puck didn't think he'd be able to live with himself.

Mr Schuester laughed and handed the sheaf of papers to Brittany and Santana to pass around. 'I guess you'll learn. It's a good opportunity for you to rely on your French partners to help you with pronunciation.'

Hmmm. Slowly, the seed of a plan was germinating in Rachel's mind.

fifteen

Choir room, Wednesday after practice

After Mr Schuester disbanded practice, reminding everyone to show up for an early morning rehearsal the next day, many of the students seemed to linger in the room, reluctantly pulling on their winter coats and scarves before they had to brave the elements outside. It had started snowing, and outside, the snow glowed under the streetlights. It had been a good practice, but it was going to take some time for the two groups of kids to mesh completely, especially since they were doing a bilingual number.

Rachel grabbed her pink peacoat and matching fluffy knit hat and made a beeline for Mr Schuester. Her fears about Celeste having a larger part in the mash-up than she did were all for nothing – it turned out that Mr Schuester and Monsieur Renaud had decided to make the number more of an ensemble piece, with many short solos. Normally, Rachel hated songs that didn't feature her heavily on lead vocal, but it was satisfying to know that Celeste didn't have any more lines than she did.

However, all she'd been able to think about during practice – besides how amazing it was that she had such perfect pitch, even when she was singing words she didn't understand – was that she had to break apart Finn and Celeste. It simply wasn't fair for Celeste to get everything.

Mr Schuester was discussing the practice with Monsieur Renaud at the piano, their backs turned to Rachel. She pointedly tapped him on the shoulder. 'Mr Schuester?'

Mr Schuester turned toward her. She wasn't sure why, but he always started to rub his forehead and wince when she spoke to him. Most likely, he knew that a gifted student like herself never asked the easy questions. In Rachel's mind, she was simply keeping McKinley's faculty on their toes. 'Yes, Rachel?'

'I just wanted to say that while I'm enjoying having Jean-Paul as my partner, I think it would be beneficial to all parties if I were to switch partners with Finn.' Rachel didn't see any harm in taking charge of the situation.

Mr Schuester frowned. Rachel looked so innocent in her thick navy blue turtleneck sweater dress and argyle tights, but he knew better. She didn't make any request unless it was self-serving. 'Why is that?'

She glanced at Finn, who had moved to the chair next to Celeste and was eagerly talking to her about something. 'Mainly because it's clear that Celeste and I are the respective stars of our glee clubs and can obviously relate to each other. I'm sure she could learn a lot from me.'

A funny look crossed Mr Schuester's face. Rachel quickly added, 'And I could undoubtedly learn a lot from her.'

'I see your point, but what about Jean-Paul?' Mr Schuester liked the idea of Rachel having to work with Celeste. Even he could see that some of the cross-cultural partnerships were flourishing and some were floundering. It might help to shake things up a bit. Besides, Celeste was incredibly talented. Working with her could deliver Rachel a nice serving of humble pie that she sorely needed. 'I don't want Jean-Paul to feel abandoned.'

Rachel shook her head vehemently. 'He won't. I think it's clear that he wants to be partnered with Finn.' She shrugged modestly, fingering the heart-shaped pendant hanging around her neck. 'I think he needs a male mentor.'

'All right, Rachel.' Mr Schuester nodded slowly. He could see how Rachel could be a little much for a quiet French guy like Jean-Paul. 'You can go ahead and let Celeste know that you'll be her American mentor for the rest of the visit.'

Rachel jumped and clapped her hands together. 'You're

the best, Mr Schuester!' For once, Mr Schuester was smart enough to not stand in her way. She smoothed down the sides of her dress and prepared herself to approach Celeste and Finn. They were having a conversation, or, more accurately, *Finn* was having a conversation. Celeste had a bored look on her face as she stuffed her sheet music into her sleek black messenger bag.

Rachel walked over to the two, a huge smile on her face, eager to break the good news to them.

Her timing, however, was terrible. Just as she appeared standing in front of them, Finn was saying, 'So, uh, do you want to go to the basketball mixer on Friday? As, you know, my date?'

Rachel's face turned beet red. She was too late! Finn was already asking Celeste out. There was a queasy feeling in the pit of her stomach, like the one she got when the family physician, Dr Engelhart, had to give her a shot. Even though she knew it would hurt, the sharp burst of pain still came as a surprise.

Celeste, however, seemed to welcome the intrusion. She was pulling a red-and-white-striped hat down over her ears, looking like some kind of ski bunny. She acted as if she hadn't even heard Finn's question. 'You were excellent yesterday, Rachel. You have a lovely voice.'

Rachel beamed. No compliment was too small to please her. And was Celeste really not going to respond to Finn's date request? 'And you do, too, Celeste. You are clearly very talented. Which is why I asked Mr Schuester if Finn and I could switch partners so that we could work more closely together.'

Rachel had expected a bit of resistance – why would Celeste want to abandon handsome Finn to work with a girl she had to know was her vocal rival? – but Celeste unexpectedly jumped to her feet and gave Rachel a quick hug. 'That is an excellent idea!' She glanced at Finn, who stared at Rachel with an annoyed look on his face. 'I would like very much to work with you.'

Finn crossed his arms and stared down Rachel. She tried not to look at him, but she could tell he was really pissed. 'What are you talking about? Celeste is my partner.'

Rachel glanced up to see if Quinn and the Cheerios were watching, but they'd been among the first people to leave the room when practice was over. She was safe talking to Finn, at least for now. 'Yes, but it just makes more sense this way. To have the two incredibly talented female leads . . .'

Finn stood up. Rachel could be so bossy sometimes, he always felt the need to stand up next to her to remind himself that he was six foot three and she was only, like, five foot two. He touched her arm and tried to pull her aside so that Celeste wouldn't hear. 'But where is this coming from?'

'I don't know what you mean,' Rachel said, grabbing her backpack from the floor. Even if he was annoyed with her, it was kind of nice to talk to Finn again. She missed him.

'Are you doing this to get back at me?' Finn's eyes looked confused. Rachel loved that confused look, which she used to see so often. 'You've been kind of pissed off at me all week.'

Rachel raised her chin in the air. Celeste was watching her, and she didn't want to look silly and emotional in front of her. 'I think you should mind your own business and go find your new partner, Jean-Paul.' She pointed to a corner of the room, where Jean-Paul was staring right at the group of them. He'd already put on his leather jacket and was just standing there, watching. It was kind of creepy. 'He's dying to hear all about your basketball season. I told him that you're undefeated, and he seemed impressed,' Rachel fibbed.

Celeste pulled on a pair of red gloves, looking eager to go. Rachel took her cue and grabbed Celeste's arm. 'We'll see you tomorrow,' she said to Finn, waving her fingers daintily just to show him there were no hard feelings.

Her plan had worked perfectly. If she'd learned anything from her repeated viewings of *All About Eve*, it was that it was very smart to keep your enemies – your competition for the spotlight or for matters of the heart – close at hand.

sixteen

Hallway, Wednesday after practice

Puck ambled out of the choir room after another strange Glee Club rehearsal with his characteristic swagger. No matter how eager he was to get out of practice, he didn't like to break a sweat doing anything except playing sports and maybe running from the mall security guard after slipping something expensive into his jeans. Immediately, he spotted Rielle standing in front of a glass trophy case full of jazz band awards. Yes, she was a glee nerd, but the French glee nerds were hot. And she had this kind of badass rocker-chick vibe to her. She'd played the guitar during the French kids' song, and there was nothing hotter than a chick guitar player, unless it was a naked chick guitar player. Maybe it was finally time to show her the Puckster charm.

Besides, she was talking to Artie, who was always wearing those sweater-vests that would turn off any girl, hot or not. Maybe that was mean, because Artie was a nice-enough dude, but Puck was a realist. And he knew he had a better shot with Rielle than Artie ever would.

'Whassup, Artie?' Puck said, giving him a light punch in the shoulder. He knew Artie probably liked to be treated like one of the guys every once in a while. He nodded at Rielle, who smiled faintly back. 'I was wondering if you'd mind doing me a huge solid.'

Artie tried not to wince. When he wasn't ignoring Artie, Puck had the annoying habit of punching Artie in the arm. And that was only when he needed a 'solid'. 'That depends,' Artie said.

Rielle giggled. She'd put on one of those knit ski hats with the flaps that came down over the ears, and it looked amazingly sexy on her. Puck couldn't resist giving her a wink. Her giggle was hot.

'It's not a big deal. I just know you take killer notes on everything we read in English, and I was hoping I could borrow yours for the book we're supposed to read this week.' Puck hooked his thumbs through the belt loops of his faded black jeans and casually flexed his pecs. 'I've been busy with basketball, what with our big game next week and our mixer this weekend. Oh, sorry, you probably don't know about that.'

'*Cyrano de Bergerac*,' Artie said, staring at his knees. Even when Puck was trying to be nice, he came off as a complete ass. 'And it's a play.' Of course Puck wouldn't read it. He could barely make it through class without snoring.

'Yeah, exactly. I didn't have time to do it, and I've got to get a better grade on the paper this time or I won't be able to play basketball.' Puck made a basketball shooting motion in the air, as if Artie wasn't familiar with the sport. 'Or do Glee.'

Artie squeezed his hands against the wheels of his chair. The last person he wanted to help was Puck, but he didn't want to look like a jerk in front of Rielle, who looked so cute in her brightly colored hat. She was actually kind of smiling at Puck. *Flirtatiously.* Great. 'Okay, that's fine. You can borrow them.'

'Sweet!' He punched Artie on the other shoulder. 'You saved my life, Artie.'

Artie rolled his eyes. He knew the only reason Puck was saying his name so much was to prove that he knew it. Just a couple of weeks ago, he'd called him 'Archie'. 'Meet me at my locker before school, and you can have them then. I need to finish up my paper tonight.'

'Cool.' Predictably, as soon as he'd gotten what he needed out of Artie, Puck turned to face Rielle, who was leaning against the wall. She had a cute habit of widening her eyes as she listened to people speak English, as if that made it easier to take in the foreign words. 'You've got a really nice voice. And it's cool that you play the guitar.'

Rielle actually blushed. Artie rolled his eyes. *Why do girls always fall for guys like Puck?* 'Thank you. Very much.'

Puck nodded, running a hand over his Mohawk. 'And I hear that you write music, too, and that you might need some help writing lyrics. Maybe I could give you a hand?'

Artie almost choked. Puck was going to write lyrics? How could that even be possible, unless they were about Nintendo games or MILFs?

'How did you know that I write songs?' Rielle asked, leaning back against the wall. She played with the zipper on her coat, pulling it up and down absentmindedly.

Puck looked uncomfortable, which made Artie smile. 'Yeah, Puck. How did you know that?' Artie enjoyed watching him squirm. He suspected Puck rarely had the opportunity to feel self-conscious.

'Oh, I, uh . . . I guess I kind of overheard you and Artie talking in the choir room before practice.' Puck looked down at his feet and shuffled his boots. 'I didn't mean to eavesdrop.' He looked up at Rielle with apologetic eyes. He even batted his eyelashes at her shyly. Artie thought he should be ashamed of himself.

But Rielle just tucked a lock of hair behind her ear and nodded. 'That's okay. I could use as many lyrics as I will have.' She glanced at Artie and gave him a slight smile. 'That will be great.'

Artie was too annoyed to smile at Rielle's tendency to mix up the future conditional and the future tenses. He felt like Puck had punched him in the stomach – he'd eavesdropped on them, and now he actually had the nerve to suggest that he wanted to help Rielle write lyrics, too? Artie knew what Puck *really* wanted.

'Cool.' Puck grinned and made a gun with his forefinger and thumb, and he fake-shot it at Rielle. 'We'll be in touch.' With another head bob, Puck turned and walked away. Artie hated the way Puck walked as if he were a cowboy or as if he'd just shot a man. If Artie could walk, he'd never walk like that. And 'we'll be in touch'? Puck was such a cartoon character.

When Puck was gone, Rielle turned her attention back to Artie. Her greenish-brown eyes were sparkling, which Artie really hated to attribute to Puck's presence. 'Puck seems very . . . how do you say in English? *Méprisable?*'

Artie chuckled and started to wheel himself down the hallway. His dad was probably waiting to pick him up. 'Sleazy.' He appreciated Rielle's comment, but he could tell she was kind of into Puck. What was it that girls saw in him, besides the overflowing confidence and the ripped biceps? He was lazy and mean and not very bright. Girls were supposed to be better than that. At least, Rielle was. Maybe Artie shouldn't have agreed to give Puck his notes after all.

As if she could read his mind, Rielle spoke. She was tugging on a pair of black leather gloves. 'It was very generous of you to help out a fellow club member. It was a nice thing to do.'

Okay, so Artie felt slightly better. Maybe he just had to resign himself to the fact that it was his lot in life to always be the one the cute girl admired, and liked, and talked to – while guys like Puck were the ones who actually *got* the girl. Artie was doomed to be the best friend, and that had to be enough for him.

'Would you . . .' Rielle started, then stopped. 'I mean, will you come to the mall with Kurt and Mercedes and some others? And me? To go shopping?'

God, she was cute. He did kind of want to go with all of them and hang out by the giant fountains in front of the arcade drinking smoothies and eating fries from the greasy steak sandwich stand. 'I . . . I can't,' Artie finally said. He had a lot of work to do, coming up with the perfect lyrics to a song for Rielle. He was going to spend the rest of the night in his room with his guitar and his notebook, brainstorming and coming up with something brilliant.

Rielle frowned. She looked like she wanted to say something, but she couldn't find the right words. Just wait until she saw what Artie came up with for her – this was his chance to shine. It took brains to write some good lyrics, and when it came down to brains, Puck wasn't even in the running.

seventeen

Lima Galleria Mall, late Wednesday afternoon

On any given weekday afternoon or evening, the Lima Galleria Mall was crowded with high school teenagers milling around looking for some way to pass the time, whether it involved terrorizing store owners by trying clothes on with abandon and not purchasing anything or sharing a salty, buttery pretzel from Auntie Anne's and checking out the opposite sex in the food court. Winter afternoons were the most crowded at the Galleria, and this Wednesday clusters of McKinley High kids wandered along the white marbled floors or sat on the steps around the giant dolphin fountain in the middle of the glassed-in, chlorine-scented atrium.

Kurt, having found the French girls to be extremely

interested in anything he had to say about fashion, was taking Angelique, Claire, Sophie, and Aimee on a tour of the mall, showing them the places to get the best skin moisturizer, the best T-shirts, the best boots – everything. They called him their tour guide and followed him wherever he went, flitting and giggling around him like a happy group of hummingbirds.

Mercedes, however, was being a little more serious. She was showing Marc around, determined to find him some cool outfits for his big American makeover. She hadn't told Kurt what she was doing, because he had a tendency to go overboard and she didn't want Marc to end up with a shaved head and wearing a vest and ascot combo.

Besides, she liked spending time with him by herself. He was fun, and they were having a really great time together.

The first place they hit was the new boutique, Mezzo. Mercedes had overheard the Cheerios blabbing about it, and, while they might be annoying, they always seemed to know about new and exciting places.

'*Mezzo* is Italian for "medium",' Marc said, looking up at the sign as they walked into the sleek, modern store. The walls were painted a sophisticated gray, and the dark walnut floors shone under the track lighting. Metal racks of clothing on wheels lined the walls, and uncomfortable-looking curved leather chairs were scattered around the room. Fast-paced pop music in a language even Marc didn't recognize played over the sound system.

Mercedes grabbed a silky black top from one of the racks. 'I hope that doesn't mean they only have mediums here, because no part of me is a medium.'

'Your voice is not a medium. It's an . . . uh . . . extra-large?' Marc suggested. He was wearing a black leather bomber jacket with a giant decal of a soccer ball on the back, but at least it covered his horrible plaid shirt.

Mercedes threw her head back and laughed. Only a French guy could get away with calling a girl *extra large*. 'Sounds kind of funny, but I'll take it.'

She casually headed toward the racks of men's clothing on the left side of the store. She hoped it wouldn't be awkward if she suggested some clothes to him, but he didn't seem too sensitive about it. When she'd suggested going shopping after school, he said, 'I could use some American clothes.' She hoped that didn't mean he was expecting her to take him somewhere where he could buy Yankees jerseys.

She grabbed a simple black button-down shirt with some black embroidery on the pocket from the rack. 'I can totally see you in this.' Yeah, if she squinted her eyes and pretended she couldn't see his terrible too-short blue jeans that were way too blue and his bright plaid shirt.

'Yes?' Marc held it up to his chest, covering up his shiny jacket. He immediately looked ten times better. 'I will try it on?'

'We'll find you a bunch of things to try on.' Mercedes

loved shopping, and it was even better to do it with someone else. She grabbed a pair of dark jeans from a stack. She was amazing at guessing people's sizes. 'It's more fun that way. Look at these jeans. They are so fly.'

'That is a good thing?' Marc asked, laughing, as he ran his fingers over a rack of sweaters. He had really nice teeth.

'Exactly.' Mercedes grabbed a charcoal-gray sweater and checked out the label. 'Like, you might say, "That Mercedes Jones is so fly."'

Marc nodded thoughtfully. He glanced at the price tag on a pair of black dress pants, then threw them over his shoulder. 'Or, that Puck kid *thinks* he is so fly.'

Mercedes pointed a finger at him. 'Damn, you got it.' Mercedes shook her head as she thumbed through a stack of T-shirts. She was pretty sure Marc was a size medium – all those French kids were pretty skinny. '*Man-whore* is another word you could use about Puck.'

'That is funny. Gerard, his partner, is also a man-whore. He has, like, eight girlfriends.' Marc grabbed a white T-shirt that had a picture of New Kids on the Block on it. Mercedes gently took it from his hand and put it back on the table.

'Really?' Mercedes wrinkled her nose. Gerard was kind of cute, but she didn't dig on short guys. But maybe it was that same overconfidence that somehow made Puck get all the girls, despite his serious shortcomings. 'Maybe that's why they don't get along.'

'I think I am at capacity. Where do you think I go to

try these on?' Marc asked, holding up his arms. They were draped with clothing. Mercedes wondered if he just liked to try on clothes or if he also had a credit card at the ready, too.

Mercedes glanced around. A skinny saleslady who resembled a contestant from *America's Next Top Model* gave them the stink eye from across the room. Mercedes headed toward an open doorway off to the side, right next to a rack of men's boxer briefs. As an inveterate mall shopper, she instinctively knew where to find the fitting rooms. She tried not to look at the underwear as she pointed the way to Marc.

'Don't forget, you have to show me every outfit, even if you hate it,' Mercedes reminded him as he ducked behind a black curtain into one of the stalls. She leaned against a rack of unwanted clothing.

'Hey, why are those Cheerio girls so odd?' Marc asked from inside his stall. She could hear him taking off his clothes, which made her wonder if he had a good body. She bet he did, even if he was kind of skinny. 'They act like they are movie stars.'

Mercedes glanced at herself in the mirror. In her slouchy teal-and-black-striped sweater and wide-leg jeans, with a gold scarf holding back her hair, she knew she looked good. 'I guess they kind of *are* the closest thing Lima has to movie stars. We don't have too much excitement around here, so everyone pays attention to them.'

'Don't they know they look funny in those costumes they wear?'

'I think that they think they look awesome.' Was it always the skinny blond girls who ruled? 'Who are the popular kids in your group? Celeste?'

'Yes, Celeste is popular. Rielle is cool, too.' Marc stepped out from behind the black curtain. He looked completely different in the new pair of jeans – they fell at just the right point over his shoes, much better than jeans that showed off his white socks. With the black button-down, he looked hot. Mercedes gave him the thumbs-up, proud of her work already. 'Does popular just mean having a lot of friends?'

Mercedes thumbed through the rack of rejected clothes, straightening the shirts on their hangers. 'No, popular means when you have a party, everyone wants to go to it, but you don't let them. Like the Basketball-Cheerios mixer on Friday night.'

'Sounds like a boring party. Those Cheerios don't have much to say.' Marc grinned deviously before ducking back behind the curtain. 'Will they wear their stupid costumes?'

Mercedes leaned against the wall and checked her phone for texts. They were supposed to meet up with Kurt and his clique of French followers for frozen yogurt. But as she thumbed through her phone, she caught sight of Brittany and Santana walking through the door of Mezzo. They were each carrying shopping bags from another store, and they strode through Mezzo as if they already knew what they were looking for. They quickly grabbed a couple of dresses each and swept into the dressing-room area. The skinny saleswoman who had snubbed Mercedes and Marc now greeted them both by name. *Typical*, Mercedes thought.

They seemed shocked to see Mercedes standing at the door to the dressing room, as if it were unimaginable that she might shop at the same place they did. Santana held a hanger with an elegant black strapless dress on her finger. Mercedes could see the tag on it read SIZE 4, which made her want to never eat a piece of pizza again. 'Hey, guys,' Mercedes said cheerfully, determined to rise above their snobby attitudes.

Santana didn't return the cheerful tone. Instead, her voice was low and bored-sounding, as if to convey her extreme disinterest in Mercedes. 'What are you doing here? And where's your dirty French lover?'

'The one with the fugly clothes,' Brittany added, as if Mercedes didn't know whom they were so crudely refer-ring to.

Mercedes's stomach dropped. She prayed Marc was too busy buttoning up to hear the girls, but their voices were loud and seemed to carry halfway through the store. 'He's right inside,' she whispered, gesturing to the fitting room.

'So? He probably knows he has fugly clothes.' Santana pushed aside a curtain and carelessly hung her clothes on the hook. One of the expensive-looking dresses slid to the floor, making a red silky puddle.

'What is wrong with you people?' Mercedes demanded. Her whole face felt hot. It was one thing for the Cheerios to be insensitive, but it was another for them to be cruel. 'Did Coach Sylvester not let you eat today?'

'What's *your* problem?' Santana asked, holding the black dress in front of her body and eyeing herself in the full-length three-way mirror. Mercedes was so high-maintenance.

'In addition to being bitchy, you guys are bad hosts. You're all so self-involved that it's no wonder you don't even realize what a cool opportunity this exchange really is.' Mercedes put her hand on her hip. It felt good to go off on these girls. 'And where are your French partners, anyway? Mr Schu is going to be upset when he realizes you've ditched them. *Again.*'

Santana rolled her eyes and slipped into her fitting room. 'And you'll be quick to tell him, I'm sure.'

'I don't trust them. They have really weird accents, which make me forget where I am,' Brittany finally spoke up in her soft, babylike voice.

'Yeah, we need to forget Glee for now and focus on the Cheerios number,' Santana said.

'You're *ditching* Glee?' Mercedes wrinkled her nose in disgust. Not that she was surprised. She knew that deep down, the two of them loved Glee as much as everyone else in the club, but they always felt the need to lash out against it because it wasn't 'cool' enough. And she knew their reputations meant everything to them. 'We need you, too.'

'Too bad there aren't more of us to go around.' Santana smiled sweetly at Mercedes. She stepped out of her stall wearing a skintight red dress that hugged every inch of her body. She turned in the three-way mirror, and suddenly Mercedes saw three of her. It was like she was stuck in a nightmare.

'We have to look hot for the party,' Brittany added, her voice muffled from behind her curtain as she pulled something over her head. 'See you there!'

Santana giggled as she fixed her hair in the mirror. 'Um, Britt. It's a Basketball-Cheerios mixer. She's not going to be there.'

'Oh.' It sounded like Brittany was stuck inside some piece of clothing, but neither Santana nor the saleswoman bothered to check in on her. 'Well, then, see you . . . some other time.'

'Maybe.' Santana pulled the curtains closed behind her, and Mercedes sighed with relief. She took a series of deep breaths, like she often had to do after an encounter with Rachel. She was not going to let those airheads get to her. But then she heard the sound of a curtain sliding aside, and there stood Marc, back in his original clothes. A few articles of clothing were slung over his arm, but he wasn't smiling. She'd almost forgotten that he was there.

'I am so sorry.' Mercedes grabbed his arm and pulled him out of the dressing room. If *she* felt bad about the Cheerios' ambush, she could only imagine how he felt. She was used to the Cheerios' rudeness, but maybe they didn't have bitchy cheerleaders in France. 'Those girls are completely terrible.'

Marc shrugged, but Mercedes could tell from the way his half-smile didn't reach his eyes that his feelings were really hurt. 'You don't need to apologize.' He held up his new clothes. 'But I think I might like to show up at this party of theirs on Friday – what is the word for showing up? Without an invitation?'

'Crashing.' She tried to imagine the look on Santana's face if some Glee kids showed up at the almighty Basketball-Cheerios mixer. It would be priceless. 'You want to crash their party?'

Marc grinned as he headed for the checkout counter. He handed a couple of shirts and the pair of jeans to the saleswoman, who looked pleasantly surprised. She was probably used to teenagers leaving all the clothes in a wad in the dressing rooms or stuffing them into their backpacks. 'I have some new, not fuggee clothing now, and I have a feeling it would ruin their night.'

Mercedes couldn't help smiling. Who said that only Cheerios could have fun?

eighteen

Choir room, Thursday morning

Mr Schuester sat on a stool and anxiously shuffled through some sheet music as the Glee kids and their French counterparts slowly filed into the choir room for morning practice. Many of them were carrying thermoses of coffee or white cardboard cups from the local coffee shop – whatever it took to keep them awake and focused. Mr Schuester and Monsieur Renaud had decided to call the morning rehearsals because halfway through practice the previous day, it had become clear that it was going to take a little more time for the groups to mesh. The clubs didn't sound terrible together, just . . . well . . . okay. And Mr Schuester had a hard time settling for *okay*.

He glanced up at Rachel, who was still wearing her puffy pink ski jacket and a pair of white mittens that matched the stocking cap on her head. She was sitting next to Celeste, who was smiling and nodding. 'It was an amazing experience working in Paris,' Celeste was saying. 'I was Street Urchin Number 1, and I only had two lines, but they were important ones.'

Rachel unzipped her coat and slid it over the back of her chair. She had a look in her eyes that Mr Schuester recognized – it was her Jealous Death Stare. He'd seen it a few times, namely, when he'd given a solo to Tina or to Mercedes instead of to Rachel, but he'd never seen it so concentrated, so pure. *Uh-oh*. 'I didn't realize Paris had a renowned musical theater scene,' she said curtly.

Celeste settled back in her chair, winding a curl of blond hair around her index finger. 'Americans never know what's going on in Europe,' she answered politely.

Maybe he shouldn't have let Rachel become Celeste's mentor. He didn't want Celeste suddenly disappearing in the night. They needed her.

Maybe this whole mentor thing had been nothing but a huge mistake. Instead of bringing kids together, it seemed like it was creating new divisions. Rachel seemed flustered in a way she never was – and why wasn't she talking to Finn? Tina and Artie, who were usually inseparable, were now sitting at opposite sides of the room, not even looking at each other.

Mr Schuester ran his hand over his forehead. He really hoped they could get it together in time. The Glee number really had to stand out against the other numbers – especially whatever crazy spectacle Sue Sylvester was cooking up with her Cheerios. He hadn't said anything about it to Philippe yet, but he was kind of hoping that if they impressed Superintendant Doherty enough, extra budget money could be put toward a visit to Lycée de Lyon in France for his Glee Club. Minus Rachel's supposed trip to Paris as an infant, none of them had been to Europe before, and it would do them good to see the world outside of Lima, Ohio.

But for that to even be a possibility, he had to rally everyone. Make the kids focus. Each and every member of the clubs needed to perform at his or her absolute best in order to make this performance great.

'Mr Schuester, are we going to get started?' Rachel was standing in front of him, an expectant look on her face.

Mr Schuester glanced at the clock. He had completely spaced out. 'Where is everybody?' It was ten minutes after start time, and the room felt only half full. Santana and Brittany were nowhere to be found – typical that they would skip together. Quinn was also absent, though maybe she deserved a few free passes. It couldn't be easy to be a pregnant high school student. And although Mr Schuester didn't want to admit it, he did feel a tiny bit responsible for some of her stress. His ex, Terri, had practically offered to buy Quinn's baby from her. That had been . . . awkward. The small French baritone – Gerard, right? – was also MIA, even though Puck was present. He had a Sausage McMuffin lying on its wrapper on his lap, and he was talking fervently to Rielle.

'They microwave the egg first – that's the key,' he explained, holding up the sandwich for her to admire. 'That's how the egg gets so evenly shaped.'

'That is so interesting,' Rielle said, glancing down at her boots.

Artie was sitting on the other side of Rielle, reading over some homework and looking miserable. Mr Schuester shook his head and approached them, the wet bottoms of his shoes – he always forgot to wear his snow boots – squeaking against the linoleum floor.

'Puck, I ran into Mr Figgins in the parking lot this morning.' He thought Puck was a good kid, deep inside, but just a little misguided and very lazy. He'd really hoped that hanging out with Glee Club would help him learn that there were more important things in the world than how many underclassmen wet their pants when he spoke to them. 'He told me that if you don't raise your English grade, you won't be able to perform in the show. You have a paper due tomorrow for Mr Horn – will you be sure to get it in on time? He's agreed to grade it right away.'

'No sweat, Mr Schu. I've got it covered.' Puck took a giant bite of his egg sandwich. He was brimming with self-confidence. 'My man Artie is lending me his *Cyrano* notes.'

Mr Schuester patted Artie on the back. 'Thanks, Artie, for helping out a friend in need.' Artie was a good kid, through and through. He was like a rock, always steady, never disappointing.

'Right.' Artie reached into his backpack and distractedly handed his English notebook to Puck. He wondered if Puck would remember that Mr Schuester had called the two of them friends the next time Puck and his gang were looking for someone to discard their slushies on.

'Thanks, man. I owe you one.' Puck held his hand up for a high five. It was greasy from the McMuffin.

Artie smiled weakly and slapped Puck's hand. Rielle was watching, and he wanted to hide his annoyance. Puck left a greasy smear on the cover of the notebook. Perfect.

'All right, everyone. Let's go ahead and get started!' Mr Schuester called out, bringing everyone to the front of the room. Once they started singing, things looked up. They were missing the Cheerios' sopranos, but Angelique, Aimee, and Claire had strong voices that made up for the loss. Monsieur Renaud seemed bothered by Gerard's absence – what could he be doing? – but Puck's and Artie's voices fleshed out the male vocals.

The only real problem, Mr Schuester hated to admit as he sat in a chair and listened, was Rachel.

She just wouldn't stay still, which normally wasn't a problem, but today she seemed to be weaving in and out among the others while she sang. Not to try to include them in the song or fire up the crowd, but to follow Celeste. When Celeste sang a line, Rachel was standing right behind her, singing just a little bit louder. At first Celeste seemed to ignore it, but before long, *she* was singing even louder to compensate. By the end of practice, Rachel and Celeste were practically elbowing each other out of the way, trying to get to center stage.

It would have been comical if the show weren't so important to Mr Schuester. But this was pretty ridiculous. 'Okay, everyone. Good practice. I'll see you all after school. If anyone sees the Cheerios and the other absent members, please remind them about rehearsal.' He cleared his throat. 'Rachel, can you stay back a minute?'

'I'll be right there,' Rachel called to her new partner, Celeste, who grabbed her things and headed into the hallway. *Celeste*. She was a force to be reckoned with. Rachel hadn't expected to encounter anyone else her age who had the same combination of excellent vocal training and natural talent as herself – at least, not in Lima. But Celeste was good. Very good. 'Yes, Mr Schuester? If this is about increasing my role in the number, you know I'm all for it. I really think—'

'No, Rachel.' Mr Schuester adjusted his tie as he watched everyone else clear from the room. He was always careful not to embarrass his students in front of their peers. 'It's about your attitude.'

'My attitude?' Rachel bristled. Her attitude was exemplary, she knew. If only the others were willing to give their all for every single song like she was, maybe they wouldn't need double rehearsals. 'What do you mean?'

'I mean that you need to tone it down.' Mr Schuester scratched his head. He'd woken up too late to have breakfast that morning, and his stomach rumbled ominously. He needed to get down to the cafeteria snack bar and grab a bagel. 'You know you're a great singer, but there's room for more than one star in this performance.'

Rachel's mouth opened wide. 'I disagree,' she announced pointedly. She was the only star, and there was only room for her.

'This performance is supposed to be about unity and about coming together.' Mr Schuester sighed and sank down onto the piano bench. Maybe if he was physically seeing eye to eye with her, it would be easier to convince her. 'I need you to find a way to work with everyone else. It's not always all about you, Rachel.'

Rachel pressed her lips together. Mr Schuester's serious lack of experience coaching talented youths was always clouding his judgment. Any seasoned coach would realize that Rachel's voice was the key to the entire performance, Celeste or no Celeste.

'Do you understand?' His eyes were annoyingly insistent.

'Perfectly.' Rachel stuck her nose in the air and spun on a heel. She gathered her things and headed for the door. 'I understand that you're so set on destroying my career it doesn't even matter if the group suffers because of it.'

'Rachel!' Mr Schuester called, but she was already out the door.

Now that he was watching her, she'd just have to be a little more subtle about putting Celeste in her place. Up ahead in the hallway, she saw Celeste giggling and talking with some other French kids. For a moment, Rachel wondered if she was overreacting. Celeste was a nice person, after all, and a very talented singer.

That didn't mean she didn't have any weaknesses.

Rachel skipped up to Celeste, keeping a cheerful smile on her face. 'Would you like to get an orange juice in the cafeteria before classes start?' Rachel asked. 'I feel that drinking orange juice – with lots of pulp – every morning strengthens my vocal cords throughout the day.'

'Really?' Celeste asked, stepping away from Claire and Nicholas and falling in step with Rachel. 'I always rely on herbal teas and honey.'

'I always drink a cup of chamomile the night before any performance.' Rachel found it easier to walk through

176

the crowded hallways with Celeste at her side – all the boys seemed to take a step back to get a better look at her. In her white T-shirt dress, gray leggings, and tall black boots, it was no wonder Celeste was gathering attention. Rachel tried to focus on more important things, such as her plan. 'What else do you do to get ready for a performance?' she asked, trying to sound as if her interest were purely professional.

What was the harm in gathering a little information?

nineteen

Cafeteria, Thursday lunch

Thursday was Indian day, and the crowded cafeteria was filled with various conflicting smells. Rachel and Celeste picked up their warm-from-the-dishwasher trays and stood in the hot-food line, peering nervously through the glass. Rachel slid her tray along the metal rails. 'Rice, please,' she said to the bored-looking cafeteria lady who was holding a spoon the size of a small shovel.

'What is this one?' Celeste asked, pointing a finger toward a vat of soupy, dark green mush. She wrinkled her perfect little nose. If Rachel had worn a white dress to school, she would have been slushied in a matter of minutes. Maybe Celeste would drop some Indian food on it – not that Rachel was wishing her any ill will.

'I think it's *palak paneer*,' Rachel answered proudly. She and her dads were devoted to takeout, and Bombay Paradise was high on their list of to-go places. This food, however, didn't look anything like the dishes at Bombay Paradise. It looked more like Bombay Purgatory.

Rachel and Celeste both decided instead on the *aloo matar*, a mixture of potatoes and peas that looked fairly innocuous. But by the time they got to the end of the line, both their heads were swimming from the overheated lunchroom – the radiators were hissing and spewing heat into the crowded room – combined with the heavy odors of Indian food.

'Do you . . . want to find somewhere else to eat?' Rachel asked Celeste. Rachel felt slightly faint. The room felt like a smelly sauna that people had been cooking in.

'That is a very good idea.' Celeste blew a strand of blond hair out of her face and followed Rachel as she wove her way around the crowded tables. The jocks were already flicking bits of curried cauliflower against the huge plate-glass windows that looked out on the snowdrifts in the courtyard. Rachel quickly navigated her way to the set of double doors at the far side of the room. Normally, carrying a full tray of food through the cafeteria was practically an invitation for someone to trip her, but Celeste's presence was like a blessing in disguise.

'We could sit on the bleachers in the gym,' Rachel suggested suddenly. 'The basketball team sometimes has extra practices during lunch in the days leading up to important games, and they've got a big game against Central Valley High on Monday.' Rachel knew she was probably just torturing herself, but she wanted to see Finn. Even if she couldn't really talk to him, it would be nice to *see* him.

Although – Quinn and the Cheerios had bailed on practice that morning. They'd broken the deal first. Rachel's heart leaped. It was over. She could talk to Finn again.

Celeste shrugged. Rachel had expected her to sound a little more excited about the prospect of seeing Finn at practice, especially after their gooey flirtation at practice just the other day. She must be trying to hide her feelings for him from Rachel.

'That's fine.'

The girls made their way down the deserted hallways to the gym. A few other students, bored with the cafeteria or interested in watching sweaty guys scramble for the basketball, were perched on the bleachers.

Rachel and Celeste carefully climbed a few rows before sitting down with their trays on their laps. The basketball team was running a layup drill at one end of the court. Each player shot a layup, then quickly ran to the other basket and stood in line to shoot a foul shot. Rachel spotted Finn, standing in line under the basket, eating a granola bar while he waited for his turn. He had on a faded blue McKinley High Athletics T-shirt that looked like it had been through the wash a million times. It probably was as thin as tissue paper.

'Isn't that Gerard?' Rachel asked suddenly. A short boy rushed toward the basket and made an effortless layup before high-fiving a couple of the other guys and dashing to the other end of the court.

Celeste giggled and stabbed a curried potato with her fork. She was staring at the long, triangular pennants hanging from the walls, announcing McKinley High's past championship basketball, girls' swim, and cheerleading teams. There were no football pennants, as the team was notoriously awful. 'Yes. He must wish he could be a basketball player.'

From the court, Finn finally looked up at the girls as he stood in line to make a foul shot. Rachel's heart almost stopped. Even in his sweaty gym clothes, with his hair standing up, he was gorgeous. She held her breath as he smiled and lifted his hand to wave.

But . . . in the same way Rachel could tell when the applause was meant especially for her, she could tell that the wave was *not* meant for her. She looked over at Celeste, who was pushing her food around her plate and not even looking at Finn. It was Celeste whom Finn was smiling at.

Rachel bit her lips, which were terribly dry because one of the Cheerios had grabbed her lip gloss that morning and flushed it down the toilet. Finn couldn't still be mad at her for switching partners, could he? He couldn't like Celeste *that* much – they'd only just met! And she was going back to France in about seventy-two hours. It was ridiculous.

Celeste glanced over at Rachel and set down her fork. She opened her tiny carton of milk and took a sip. 'Is Finn a . . . typical American boy?'

Rachel stared down at Finn. In a way, he was. 'I don't know. He cares about sports and video games and his family and friends. He can eat four whole hot dogs without getting a stomachache.' But he was so much more than that. Finn actually liked being in Glee Club, and he stood up for what he believed in, even if it didn't make him popular with his friends. 'No,' she said finally. 'Not really. What is a typical French boy like?'

Celeste smiled. She had unbearably straight teeth. 'I guess it is a hard question. But French boys are very complicated. They are not very, um . . .' She searched for the right word. 'Straightforward? They are very secretive and don't talk about their feelings, ever, but they get annoyed when you can't read their minds.'

'I guess American boys don't always talk about their feelings, either. Sometimes they get sick of you before you even have any idea something is wrong.' Rachel stared down at Finn. Talking about him to Celeste was making her slightly miserable, yet she felt like she couldn't stop.

Celeste glanced from Rachel to Finn and back again. The basketball coach tweeted his whistle and gathered the boys together. She set down her fork. 'Wait . . . were you and Finn . . . boyfriend and girlfriend?'

Rachel blushed. She imagined Celeste asking her questions about Finn – like what was his favorite ice cream (chocolate-chip cookie dough) or his favorite movie (*Field of Dreams*, although he'd say *Transformers* if asked). She didn't like the way this conversation was going. It was Rachel who was supposed to be discovering things about Celeste, not the other way around. 'Briefly.' Rachel quickly stuffed a forkful of *aloo matar* into her mouth to avoid further questioning.

'I thought there was something between you.' Celeste leaned back, her blue eyes sparkling. She took a napkin and dabbed at the corners of her mouth delicately. 'Finn is nice, but . . . I guess I just do not get what the big deal is about him.' She shrugged demurely, as if she'd just said she didn't understand what the big deal $e=mc^2$ was.

Rachel almost dropped her fork. She turned to face Celeste, her tray almost sliding off her lap. *'What?'*

Celeste shrugged and stared thoughtfully into the air. Her lips were pink and glossy and perfect. 'I don't think he's all that great.'

Rachel blinked. Was something getting lost in translation here? How could Celeste not think Finn was great? He was tall and classically handsome, yet his big brown eyes were puppy-dog sweet. 'You mean, you don't like him?'

'He's nice,' Celeste repeated, but it was clear she was just being diplomatic. Suddenly, Rachel liked Celeste a thousand times better. 'And I wanted to, you know, try him out? I heard that American boys were much more simple and sweet.'

'Try him out,' Rachel repeated. She was still having trouble processing, but she was finally getting it. Celeste was a threat only to Rachel's career, *not* her love life. She felt like a huge weight had been lifted from her shoulders.

'He's very attractive, to be sure. But he is always staring at me and does not have much to say.' Celeste popped a forkful of *aloo matar* into her mouth. 'He's a little strange, no? A little like a . . . how do you say? Oaf?' A pea escaped from her fork and dropped down the front of her white dress, leaving a trail of yellow curry sauce. *'Merde.'*

'Yes,' Rachel agreed fondly. She actually felt bad that Celeste had spilled on herself, and she quickly dabbed her napkin with her sparkling water and handed it to her partner. 'He is like an oaf.' Her day seemed that much brighter. Celeste did not like Finn after all. Rachel had nothing to worry about!

'Also, I have decided to swear off boys. They always are a disappointment.' Celeste smiled a little sadly as she patted at the curry sauce on her dress. Almost as if she were blessed, it disappeared. 'Especially after my last boyfriend. He cheated on me, can you believe?'

Rachel's eyes widened. How could anyone cheat on Celeste? She was so beautiful, and talented, and blond. 'Really?'

'Really.' Celeste set her tray aside and leaned back against the bleachers. Her white dress looked perfect again. 'I am finished. Besides, boys only distract a girl from her career, which is definitely more important. Who has the time to get all obsessed with some silly boy and still develop her talent?'

Rachel couldn't believe what she was hearing. She set her tray aside as well. Suddenly, she didn't even care that Finn had made an amazing three-point shot practically from half-court. 'I completely agree with you.'

'You do?' Celeste looked at Rachel, and a renewed respect for each other dawned in their eyes. Maybe they weren't so different after all.

'Yes!' Rachel exclaimed. She tugged her corduroy skirt farther down over her knees when she noticed that the nerdy water boy was staring up at them. 'Barbra Streisand wouldn't be where she is today if she fell all head over heels for some boy in high school. She knew her priorities, and she wouldn't let anyone distract her from her dreams!'

'Or Edith Piaf,' Celeste continued, twirling her silver bangle around her delicate wrist. 'She was very dedicated to her path, and she would not let anyone cheat on her.' Her face flushed as she spoke, as if she was still angry – and hurt – that her ex-boyfriend had actually cheated on her. Rachel felt a rush of sympathy for her. She wanted to give her a hug. *Boys!*

'I'm really glad we're partners,' Celeste said suddenly. Her blue eyes looked relaxed and happy, and Rachel felt her heart melting. 'I really like you, and I really like McKinley High.'

Rachel beamed. She was used to people telling her she was bossy or a control freak. Even though she thought of the other Glee kids as friends – most of them – she never felt like they *understood* her. They always thought she was weird for taking things too seriously. And here was Celeste, her almost exact French counterpart – talented, motivated, and fairly attractive.

Okay, so Celeste was extremely attractive. But Rachel knew she had her moments, too, even if no one else seemed to appreciate them.

Rachel looked down at her tray of half-eaten Indian food. Then she glanced down at the court. Finn and the other basketball guys were doing some sort of passing drill. His hair was sweatier now, but there was still something undeniably appealing about him. What Celeste called 'oafish' Rachel preferred to think of as 'boyish charm'. She took a deep breath. Part of her wanted to sit and watch Finn all day.

But what good would that do? He'd decided he didn't want to be with her, and if Rachel kept pining over him, she was bound to get distracted from what was really important. Rachel pushed Finn to the back of her mind. 'I think the choir room might be empty right now – do you want to go squeeze in another quick practice?'

Rachel was not surprised to hear Celeste squeal in excitement. 'Yes, of course. Let us go.' She *was* the French Rachel, after all.

It looked like it could be the beginning of a beautiful friendship.

twenty

McKinley High hallway, Thursday afternoon

Rachel nearly skipped down the hallway on her way to algebra, her last class of the day. She and Celeste had had an excellent practice together – somehow, when it was just the two of them, Celeste was much less intimidating. Or maybe it was because Rachel knew she wasn't interested in Finn anymore. Sure, she had an incredible voice and had a face that Rachel suspected was annoyingly photogenic. But Rachel felt much safer, especially knowing that Celeste would be leaving in a matter of days. Rachel might even miss her.

Either way, Rachel's government class flew by, with Rachel barely listening as Mr Prospero lectured on the doctrine of the separation of powers. It didn't even bother

her when she felt a couple of spit wads zing past her ear – those jocks in the last row could throw as many as they wanted (they had terrible aim, anyway) because she was too focused on the future. And Rachel's future was nothing if not sunny and bright.

Rachel's good mood came to an abrupt end after class when she saw three familiar girls headed toward the back entrance of the school, tugging on thick winter coats. Carrying her bricklike math textbook in her arms like a shield, she managed to rush down the hallway and make it to the glass doors before the girls had left, raising only a few curious glances from the students in the hallway as she elbowed past them.

'Where do you think you're going?' Rachel demanded, staring down Quinn, Santana, and Brittany. She felt much more confident now for some reason. Maybe it was realizing that Celeste wasn't an enemy, that there were other girls out there who took their careers as seriously as she did.

·'To get nonfat lattes.' Brittany zipped up her coat over a strand of her long blond hair. 'Ouch!' She tried to get the zipper down, but it was stuck. Santana leaned over to help, rolling her eyes.

Quinn grabbed her car keys from the pocket of her navy blue peacoat. The big navy buttons had tiny etchings of anchors on them. Even though her protruding abdomen made it impossible for her to fasten them, everything about Quinn still seemed perfectly neat and proper. 'We don't have to answer to you.'

Rachel felt like throwing her math book at one of them – probably Quinn – but instead she kept it clutched to her chest. 'What happened to our deal? You weren't at Glee practice this morning, and that's a clear violation of our agreement. The only reason I agreed to not tell Figgins about your ditching was because Glee needs you. And you don't seem to care.'

Quinn casually pulled a pair of tan leather gloves from her backpack and slid her thin hands into them. As usual, she looked elegant and chic, and next to her, Rachel looked like a spoiled child threatening to tattle. 'You might remember that your part of the deal included not talking to Finn.'

'And yesterday in practice, you were all over him like a cheap suit.' Santana wrapped a scarf around her neck. 'A very cheap suit.'

Quinn smiled. Even though she looked like she could be on the cover of a magazine, sweet and wholesome, every time her mouth opened something mean seemed to come out. 'A blatant violation of your part of the bargain.'

Rachel felt her face heat up. She took a step backward. It was like they had eyes in the backs of their heads, beneath their perfectly perky ponytails. 'That's ridiculous! I asked him one question . . . about Celeste's career!'

'A deal's a deal, and you're the one who broke it.' Santana slid a tube of pink lip gloss over her lips, leaving a bubblegum shine behind. 'But seriously, I'm getting a caffeine headache, so we're going to go.'

Without another look at Rachel, the three girls disappeared out the door into the cold. Snow was falling quickly, and before they were ten steps from the door, Rachel couldn't even identify them. Not that they would have cared – they clearly thought they were so important to this school that they could come and go as they pleased. *What brats!* She should have known better than to try to reason with them. It was stupid to think they could uphold their part of a bargain, but all she wanted was for Glee to have a chance. Too late for that.

And so she didn't feel one bit guilty as she stormed past the door to the math room and straight to Principal Figgins's office. He, for one, would care.

Rachel was so focused on what she was going to say to Figgins that she almost passed the plate-glass wall of the guidance counselor's office without thinking twice about the familiar head of blond, curly hair sitting opposite Miss Pillsbury. Almost. But even her determination to snitch on Quinn and the Cheerios couldn't completely block her natural curiosity, and Rachel stopped in her tracks.

The hair, of course, belonged to Celeste, her new partner, sitting there, chatting with Miss Pillsbury. The guidance counselor was wearing a navy blue polka-dotted shirt with a tiny bow at the neck, and she was nodding and listening as Celeste talked animatedly. A full bottle of Windex and a roll of paper towels sat at the corner of her desk. For a moment, Rachel considered pressing her ear to the glass to see if she could hear anything, but she knew Miss Pillsbury was ultrasensitive about anyone touching the glass. What could Celeste possibly need guidance about? She didn't even go to *school* here. Very weird.

But Rachel had more important things to think about. She was on a mission to punish Quinn and the Cheerios for abandoning Glee, and everything else could wait.

twenty-one

Auditorium, Cheerios practice, Thursday after school

'Come on, people – I've seen morphine-addicted sloths with more pep than this. Step it up!' Coach Sylvester bellowed into her red plastic bullhorn. The Cheerios were practicing for their Multicultural Show routine in the auditorium, and Coach Sylvester's words echoed menacingly against the acoustic tiles lining the walls. Whenever she was coaching, she had a slightly crazy gleam in her eyes.

The Cheerios started their routine again, this time with more energy. They were wearing their crisp red-and-white Cheerios outfits, and their routine had a distinctly all-American flavor to it, even though it was set to a ridiculously fast version of 'It's a Small World' with a techno backbeat.

'With energy this time!' The routine, while technically challenging, seemed a little shallow. It basically involved a lot of sexy, robotlike dance moves. Sue Sylvester, not surprisingly, was missing the whole purpose of the Multicultural Fair and Multicultural Week, both of which were designed to celebrate different cultures and to promote a better understanding of the power of global unity. 'Remember, I chose this song because the only world where all cultures get along is one in which everyone is made of plastic and wears glitter. Now move it, you talentless teenage drones!'

The school district's politically correct reasoning for having a Multicultural Fair in the first place made her ill, and she planned on using her Cheerios to prove a point. She'd choreographed an ironically peppy routine to show how ridiculous the idea of cultural unity was in the first place.

Although Coach Sylvester had thrown the routine together just yesterday, her Cheerios were such talented performers – who simultaneously were terrified of her and would take a bullet for her, which was exactly the way she wanted it – that they could easily be whipped into shape in just a few days. Besides, with her best athletes, Santana and Brittany, as the centerpieces of the routine, performing all the most complicated dance moves, it was hard to go wrong.

Mr Schuester poked his head through the door at the back of the auditorium. He didn't mean to spy on Sue Sylvester – something she had accused him of on many occasions – but he was looking for a few of his girls who had skipped practice. They both, coincidentally, happened to be Cheerios.

As he suspected, he quickly spotted Santana and Brittany leading the routine. Mr Schuester took a deep breath. He'd stepped out of Glee rehearsal to find them, and it didn't take him too long before he heard the thumping of the Cheerios number through the halls of the school. Even though he'd kind of expected to find the girls with Coach Sylvester, it still hurt his feelings. The girls knew how much Glee Club needed the extra funding that they could earn with a great performance at the Multicultural Fair, and yet here they were, practicing with the Cheerios, who had more money than Midas. And worse, they hadn't said a single word to him about no longer being in the Glee number.

Mr Schuester still had trouble connecting with the Cheerios. He knew they liked Glee, although they were too proud to admit it, but he also knew that Coach Sylvester demanded absolute loyalty to her squad. He hated that any student would be put in a tough spot like this, but they needed to learn that they couldn't walk away from their responsibilities without a single word.

Mr Schuester strode down the long aisle of the auditorium, all the way to the stage. Sue Sylvester, sitting in the middle of the auditorium, blew her whistle angrily as she noticed his approach.

'Is there a problem, William?' Coach Sylvester demanded through her bullhorn. 'We're in the middle of a rehearsal, and there is a treasonous stench of Camembert radiating from your greasy mop of hair. It is pungent, and it is suffocating my athletes.'

Mr Schuester glanced at her briefly. Her banana-yellow tracksuit was blinding. 'I just wanted to ask some of my Glee Club members if they were going to be joining us for rehearsal.'

Coach Sylvester was about to say something derisive to put him in his place when she realized it would be that much more priceless if it came directly from the girls. She waved her bullhorn at Santana, indicating that she was allowed to speak.

Santana reluctantly stepped forward. She wiped a bead of sweat off her forehead with the back of her hand. It was hot onstage under all the lights, which Coach Sylvester had insisted be turned on to toughen the girls up. What the hell did Mr Schuester think he was doing, storming into Cheerios practice and demanding they come back to Glee Club? Did he not understand who they were? Santana, newly appointed head Cheerio, could no more agree to go to Glee practice in front of her peers than she could admit that she actually kind of hated wearing her uniform to school every day, even if it did send a message to the rest of the student body that she deserved special treatment. 'I'm sorry, Mr Schuester.' She put her hands on her hips. She felt sorry for him, standing there in the middle of the auditorium with two dozen girls staring at him. 'But I can't leave the Cheerios.'

'Me, neither,' Brittany quickly seconded.

Mr Schuester took a deep breath. He realized that his mistake, too late, had been to confront the girls in public, in front of their friends. These were girls who took their position at the top of the McKinley High School social ladder very seriously. Of course he couldn't expect them to abandon that for the bottom-rung Glee Club. 'I'm sorry to hear that, girls.' He stepped backward and waved his hand in an 'it's okay' type of gesture. 'We'll miss you, and just remember, you're always welcome to come back and join us for the number if you choose.'

Santana bit her lip. She knew that if she'd skipped Cheerios practice to be with Glee Club, she'd be dead to Coach Sylvester. Poor Mr Schuester. He was sort of a nice guy, after all, even if he was kind of dopey.

But, still. There was no way she could do anything about it now. 'I'll remember that,' she said haughtily. She felt Coach Sylvester's eyes trained on her, searching for any sign of weakness.

Mr Schuester stopped as he passed Coach Sylvester on

his way out. Somehow, she made a polyester tracksuit look as intimidating as a full Marine uniform. 'Sue, you're a bully.'

'Offensive.' Sue shook her head slowly at him. 'If I wasn't too busy laughing at your Brillo pad of a haircut, I would consider pointing out to you that bullies are usually hiding their own insecurities behind bluster and bravado. I, on the other hand, have no insecurities to hide.' She pointed a finger at him and lowered her voice. 'And I wouldn't hold your breath waiting for my girls to come back to Glee Club. It's humanly impossible for them to choose to spend time with your group of artsy-fartsy losers while they continue to embody the physical perfection of my Cheerios squad.'

Mr Schuester knew better than to try to get the last word in on Sue Sylvester, so he simply shook his head and turned his back to her. He was sure his Glee Club could still do a great job without the Cheerios, even though they'd have to work a little bit harder.

Since when had that been a problem?

twenty-two

Parking lot, Thursday after school

Winter days in Lima were so short that by the time practices let out, it was already pitch-black outside. Not that Quinn had attended any practice that afternoon. She had been exhausted after school, so she went to the coziest place on campus she could think of – the library – to kill some time before Glee. She had accidentally fallen asleep among the stacks of dusty, dog-eared copies of *The Scarlet Letter* and woken up an hour later with drool all over the arm of her favorite blue sweater. She had actually intended to go to practice, despite the fact that the deal with Rachel was broken. Singing usually helped Quinn take her mind off all the things in her life that were barreling out of control, but

199

she hadn't been sleeping well and clearly owed herself a break. She groggily gathered her things and headed outside. The rush of cold air that hit her when she walked out the side entrance of the school felt so good that she was grateful her coat now refused to button. Her hair, slightly damp with sweat from the overheated library, immediately froze into stiff strands. Seconds later, Santana burst through the double doors shivering. She had practically negative body fat, so she frantically pulled on her red Cheerios letter jacket and was stuffing her bare hands into her pockets.

'Hey, Q. So what are you wearing to the party tomorrow?' Santana asked, stomping her feet to keep warm and nearly slipping on the sheet of ice that covered the sidewalk. The tiny beads of salt meant to melt the ice appeared to be ineffective. 'I don't want it to look like we coordinated, but we should coordinate.' Quinn was still planning to go to the party. She may not be a Cheerio anymore, but she still deserved a social life. Didn't she?

Quinn quickly scanned the student parking lot. Finn's beat-up car was still there. He must still be at Glee practice, probably fawning all over that Celeste harlot. Quinn knew it wasn't any of her business anymore whom Finn hung out with, but it was slightly humiliating to see him head-over-heels for this girl he barely knew. The Cheerios' network was a gossipy bunch, and over the past few days she'd received countless reports of how Finn practically had to wipe the drool off his face every time he talked to Celeste. He'd allegedly done five push-ups at basketball practice while she sat on his back. *Ew. How embarrassing.* Maybe the one good thing about accidentally missing Glee practice was that she didn't have to witness the flirting firsthand anymore today.

'What did you say?' Quinn asked after a moment of silence when she realized it was her turn to talk.

Santana rolled her eyes. She rolled her eyes so often that Quinn was seriously worried she'd damage her eye nerves. 'You're clearly distracted. I'll call you later tonight,' Santana said as she jogged over to the red convertible her mother occasionally let her borrow.

Quinn usually gave Santana a ride home, but she was grateful that she didn't have to today. She just wasn't in the mood to talk about how her ex-boyfriend seemed ready to tattoo the name of some French skank on his forehead, while Quinn ballooned up like that girl in *Charlie and the Chocolate Factory*.

'Later.' Quinn barely managed to give a wave to Santana because she'd seen something much more interesting. Puck was headed toward his black car, swaggering, as usual, despite the icy sidewalks. When she wanted an ego boost, Puck, who was pure libido, could usually be counted on to provide it. Even though they hadn't hooked up since their brief fling last fall (which had gotten her pregnant), he never stopped flirting with Quinn. Quinn made a beeline for his car so that by the time he got there, she was leaning seductively against the driver-side door, her arms crossed in front of her. She'd even reapplied her mint chocolate lip gloss, which she knew made Puck crave ice cream.

'Did you miss me at practice?' she asked flirtatiously. Puck had only joined Glee to watch the hot girls, she was pretty sure. Even though he had an amazingly sexy voice, she knew he wasn't in the club for his own vocal edification. He just liked to watch the Cheerios skirts swirl around their thighs as they danced.

'What . . . you weren't there?' Puck asked absentmindedly. He glanced back toward the door to the school, as if waiting for someone. He had his letterman's jacket on, with badges on the arms for football, basketball, and baseball.

Quinn suddenly felt cold, and she tried to pull her peacoat closed over her chest. What was the matter with Puck? Did she smell sweaty and nasty from the stifling library? She couldn't – she'd put on some of her powder-fresh-scented deodorant after splashing water on her face in the girls' bathroom. And besides, Puck actually *liked* the smell of her sweat – it was like some sort of aphrodisiac, and it usually made him most susceptible to her charms.

'You didn't notice?' she asked, pouting. Her breath was visible in the early evening air. Maybe he was playing hard to get. He liked to think he could torture her, too.

Puck finally smiled. He had the kind of crooked grin that her mother would have called devilish, if Quinn had ever let her parents meet him. She obviously knew better. 'I guess I was distracted.'

Quinn played with the handle of Puck's car. If she wanted to, she could lean forward and kiss him. But she didn't want to. Not yet. 'You're going to the basketball mixer tomorrow night, right?'

Puck nodded, twirling his car keys around his index finger. 'Hell, yeah. It's the place to be.'

She crossed her arms over her chest. 'Good. I bought a new dress especially for the occasion.' She looked up at him through her long dark lashes in a way that usually made him fall to his knees and beg. When she prayed every night, she thanked God for blessing her with such naturally thick lashes. She pitied girls who had to rely on mascara.

Then something strange happened. Puck . . . actually laughed. 'I'm sure you'll look hot, princess. I, however, have got another plan, and her name is Rielle.' Puck stepped forward, and while he didn't exactly push Quinn out of the way, it was clear that he expected her to move. She quickly stepped aside, her sneakers slippery against the pavement. Puck unlocked his car door and climbed in. 'But maybe if things don't work out with her, you can be my backup.' Puck didn't feel too badly about rejecting Quinn – she had already made it pretty clear that she thought he was just a 'Lima loser' when he had tried to play the baby-daddy role. She probably wanted him now only because she was jealous of Rielle. Chicks were always pulling that crap.

'I don't play backup,' Quinn said, but he'd already started the engine and pulled the door shut behind him. He backed out of his spot without looking, which was typical Puck. He gave her an irritating wink as he pulled away.

Quinn was fairly certain her face had turned a shade of purple. She was furious. Most guys would kill to have a chance with her, and no one had ever – *ever* – turned her down. At least no one else had been around to witness her humiliation. Turned down by Puck, the biggest man-slut in the tri-county area? The *father* of the baby she was carrying? So much for their incredible magnetism.

As she tried to figure out how to salvage some of her self-esteem, she spotted someone sitting on a bench near the school, hunched over a notebook. It was that dark-haired Jean-Paul kid from the French glee club. Quinn stared at him. He was cute enough, in an Edward Scissorhands kind of way, but he seemed so broody, sitting out in the cold, scribbling in his notebook. Ugh, that was so French and weird of him.

But – that didn't mean he was completely useless.

Quinn walked over to him, her sneakers slipping a few times on the ice. The closer she got, the more she realized how perfect this was. She'd been pulling her hair out with jealousy over Finn's crush on the French chick, and now Puck was trying to go European, too. (Just wait until he found out they didn't shave their legs – or armpits.) Why not give the guys a taste of their own medicine and see how they liked it when she picked a French guy to hang out with instead of them?

'Jean-Paul, right?' Quinn said when she was standing right in front of him. She turned on the Quinn Fabray thousand-watt smile, even though she couldn't imagine having to work very hard to get *this* boy's attention.

Jean-Paul looked up from his notebook. He didn't exactly seem happy to see Quinn, but he didn't look irritated at the interruption, either. He seemed mildly curious. Right now, Quinn would take that.

'Your name is . . . Quinn?' he asked, pronouncing her name like 'queen'. His voice was surprisingly deep, and the French accent was actually pretty sexy.

And she could get used to being called *queen*. 'Do you have plans for tomorrow night?' she demanded, even though it was a silly question. What kind of plans could a French exchange student have?

Jean-Paul just shook his head. Even more perfect – a man of few words.

'Now you do. You are going to a party with me. Okay?' Her 'okay' was merely to be polite – it was clear from the tone of her voice that she wasn't asking but telling him.

She was going to escort him to one of the social events of the season, and he would be suitably grateful. Who wouldn't kill to show up somewhere with Quinn Fabray at his side? Well, besides Finn and Puck, apparently.

Jean-Paul's blue-gray eyes actually showed a flicker of interest. 'Is it the party Finn will be at? The basketball one?'

Quinn blinked. That was a weird thing to ask. 'Yes.' He must have some kind of man-crush on Finn. Maybe he and Kurt could start a fan club. But whatever. He was tall and good-enough-looking, and he could serve his purpose well.

Jean-Paul nodded. He stuffed his notebook into his leather messenger bag. Quinn hoped he didn't think she was going to give him a ride back to the hotel just because she'd asked him out. She was no boy's chauffeur. 'Okay. I will come.'

'Perfect.' At least one thing was going her way. Puck wasn't the only one who knew how to make a backup plan.

twenty-three

Mr Horn's English class, Friday

Artie anxiously sat at his desk in Mr Horn's English classroom, tapping his fingers against the spokes of his wheels. At about midnight last night, he'd woken up from the middle of a dream – a really nice one, actually, where he was playing basketball and Tina was cheering him on from the bleachers – with a burst of energy. He had a great idea for a few new lyrics for Rielle, and he flicked on his bedside table lamp and reached for the notebook he always kept there. (He sometimes got inspirations from his dreams, and he liked to jot them down.) In his sleepiness, it took a few moments for him to realize he hadn't written the lyrics for Rielle in his bedside notebook – they were in his

English notebook. The very same notebook he'd given Puck.

Artie had felt sick all morning, worrying about Puck reading his lyrics and figuring out his feelings for Rielle. He cursed himself for being so stupid – but he'd been so distracted when he'd handed over the notebook to Puck, not wanting to look like a bad guy in front of Rielle. And yesterday, he'd been so busy – with practice and with a special AV Club meeting to talk about plans to record the Multicultural Show on Saturday. Then, his mother had taken the family out to El Camino, the local Mexican restaurant, for dinner to celebrate some project she'd completed at work, and Artie had finished editing his paper on *Cyrano de Bergerac* before falling into bed. (He'd written it days earlier, almost as soon as he'd read the play. What was wrong with being prepared?)

Seconds before the bell rang, Puck sidled through the door. In his torn jeans and tight black thermal T-shirt, his Mohawk getting a little long and wild, he didn't exactly look like the kind of guy who would hand in homework. Which was why it was so surprising that when he slid into the seat in front of Artie, he pulled a typed-up paper from inside Artie's notebook. He held on to the paper and dropped the notebook – which looked like it had been stuffed into his pocket at some point – onto Artie's desk. Several grease stains spotted the cover, as if he'd been eating pepperoni pizza while reading it.

'Thanks, dude.' Puck grabbed Artie's tie and tugged it in what he must have believed was an act of affection. Artie almost choked. 'Your notes really helped me get the paper done.'

'Did I hear you correctly, Mr Puckerman?' Mr Horn paused next to Puck's desk. 'Did you say you finished your paper? On time?'

Puck handed Mr Horn a sheaf of papers stapled together in the corner. 'Read it and weep, Mr Horn.' He winked over his shoulder at Artie.

'I don't believe it.' Mr Horn fanned himself with Puck's paper as if he were going to faint with shock. 'Maybe next time, Brittany, you can aspire to be more like Mr Puckerman.' Mr Horn made a notation in red pen in his grade book.

Brittany stared down at her empty desk. 'I tried to write a paper, but I had to help this squirrel outside my bedroom window find his acorns.'

The whole conversation, which normally would have amused Artie, flew over his head as he frantically paged through the notebook Puck had handed back to him. He hoped that Puck had been so busy copying his notes – Artie was fairly sure that Puck's paper simply regurgitated his notes in slightly less grammatical form – that he hadn't noticed the song lyrics. He barely knew how to read, right?

But after flipping through the notebook several times

with no luck, he paused in the middle of it. Stuck to the spiral binding were several tiny scraps of notebook paper, the kind that got left behind when sheets were torn out.

His stomach dropped. Not only had Puck *read* his lyrics . . . he'd *stolen* them? Why would he do that? He could imagine him stealing cigarettes from convenience stores, and maybe even cars from parking lots, but song lyrics from someone's notebook? Artie was used to Puck being thoughtless, but stealing his lyrics just seemed plain cruel.

Artie sunk his head into his hands. He'd worked so hard to come up with something to impress Rielle, and now he was going to end up letting her down. She was going to think he was just another guy who was trying to get in her pants.

Still furious, he poked Puck in the shoulder with his pencil. The sharp end. Puck startled awake.

'What happened to the rest of the stuff in here?' Artie demanded. He pushed his thick black glasses back into place. 'The lyrics I wrote?'

'Oh.' Puck's handsome face looked sheepish, as if he'd been caught stealing a cupcake. He squirmed in his seat. 'I kind of borrowed them. You know, to impress a girl.'

'What?' Artie hissed. He normally felt guilty talking in class, but this was an emergency.

'I don't know. Reading about Cyrano de Berg-Bergerac

210

– whatever his name is – in your notes gave me an idea.' He shrugged. His shoulders were ridiculously muscular.

'You actually read the play?' Artie was momentarily stunned.

'No, just your notes,' Puck admitted. He started chewing on the cap of his Bic pen. Artie had read once that thousands of people died every year when they accidentally choked on pen caps. Artie wasn't saying he wanted Puck to choke to death – just maybe choke a little. 'I saw your song lyrics, and I figured I could just, you know, de Bergerac Rielle.'

Rielle? Artie took off his glasses, setting them carefully on his desk, and rubbed his eyes. Of course Puck had used the lyrics to impress Rielle and not one of the mentally challenged girls he normally chased after. And of course Cyrano – the one character they read about in English class who seemed to really resonate with Artie because it addressed someone with a physical handicap – meant something totally different to someone like Puck. Puck, like the dim-witted but good-looking character Christian, could use the words of someone smarter than he was to win the love of the girl they both wanted.

Artie felt completely and totally crushed. He carefully put his glasses back on.

'If it makes you feel any better, dude, your lyrics were totally great.' Puck still looked a little guilty, but the smirk on his face showed he thought it was totally worth it.

'Rielle really loved them. She's even going to go to the basketball party with me tonight.' Puck lifted his hand up for a high five.

Artie just stared at him. If glasses could fog up with anger, his would have. 'You're joking.'

'Dude, it's not a big deal.' Puck rubbed his chin. 'I'll owe you one. Next time someone dumps a slushie on your head, I'll hand you some napkins.'

Maybe it's not a big deal to you, Artie thought. The worst part wasn't even that he wasn't going to get Rielle. He never really thought he would in the first place – even if he was a romantic, he was ultimately pragmatic. But he couldn't let *Puck* take credit for his work – Puck, who bragged that he hadn't read a single book cover to cover in two years.

Artie had to find a way to let Rielle know the lyrics were his, even if it didn't make any difference in how she felt about him. He just couldn't let her go on thinking that Puck had a soul, when he clearly didn't.

twenty-four

Luke Wainwright's house, Friday night

The Basketball-Cheerios mixer was not an officially sanctioned event, as Coach Sylvester did not approve of house parties, even though she did encourage her able-bodied Cheerios to associate with boys who were equally physically gifted. Luke Wainwright was the lucky host of the mixer this Friday night. Although he was an insignificant bench player on the basketball team, his parents took a yearly ski trip to the Poconos, and, once a year, he became a real star. Not only did his parents leave the house all to him, but he had an older brother at Ohio State who was more than willing to come home for the weekend and buy his little brother some beer, provided that Luke would introduce him to a few pretty cheerleaders.

The Wainwright house was a large McMansion at the end of a long, secluded driveway, with only a handful of neighbors. Their driveway was lined with cars, and from the outside, it looked as if every light in every window was glowing brightly. From a quarter of a mile away, one could feel the stereo beat thumping. The lack of neighbors was especially valuable, as it meant a lesser likelihood of the police arriving unexpectedly.

Finn pulled into the driveway and parked his car between a snowbank and a Mustang with the headlights still on. 'Let me get the door for you,' he said to Celeste as he got out of the car and tried to hurry to the other side. He wanted to show her that American guys were – what was it Rachel had called him one day? Chivalrous?

But she must not have heard him, because by the time he got around to the passenger-side door, Celeste was already slamming it shut. 'Thank you for the ride,' Celeste said to him, bundling her coat tighter around herself. She looked pretty, even under her bulky coat.

That's a weird thing to say, Finn thought. He wasn't just her ride – he was her date, right? Maybe she was just nervous about going to her first American party. He should really try to put her at ease. As they walked up the sidewalk to the front door, he put an arm around her shoulder. 'Do you play pool? Luke has this killer pool table in the basement.'

'Do you mean billiards?' Celeste asked, carefully stepping

up the front steps in her high heels. His arm fell off her shoulder.

'Uh, I guess?' Finn knocked on the door. He could hear thumping music coming from inside, but he felt kind of weird just opening the door and letting himself in.

'Only old men with drinking problems play billiards in France,' Celeste announced. Her cheeks were pink from the cold.

'Oh.' Finn pushed on the door, which wasn't fully latched, and it creaked open. Loud music and a burst of heat immediately washed over them. The house was packed with McKinley High students. While it was officially a mixer only for the basketball team and the Cheerios, other select people had been invited, namely pretty girls and upperclassmen who were known to also host their fair share of parties. Luke's brother, who was sitting on a couch with his arm around a Cheerio who was asking him about college football players, had filled the fridge with cans of beer, but most of the Cheerios were abstaining. They all knew Coach Sylvester had a nose like a police dog's for alcohol, and if she suspected any of her Cheerios of partaking before a major performance, she would make them rescind their uniforms and personally throw them in the incinerator.

'Can I take your coat?' Finn asked Celeste, who quickly shrugged out of her winter jacket. She looked as hot as ever in a sparkly red tank top and a pair of black jeans, but she seemed different, somehow. Quiet. What was going on with all the girls in his life all of a sudden? First Rachel completely stopped talking to him, now Celeste. 'I'm just going to put the coats in the spare room. I'll be right back.'

'Okay.' Celeste was already weaving through the crowd. A few of the French kids were in attendance as well – Gerard was surrounded by a bunch of basketball guys. He was talking animatedly, and the guys were all laughing.

When Finn came back, Celeste was sitting on a window seat, holding an open can of beer in her hand but not drinking. Finn grabbed a Gatorade from the kitchen and sat down next to her. 'So, uh . . . we have a big game against Central Valley High on Monday,' he said, searching his brain for something to say. He was psyched to be there with Celeste, who looked totally hot in her outfit. All the other guys were staring at them jealously.

But conversation with her was really hard for some reason. As Finn took a swig of his drink, he kind of wished he were talking to Rachel instead of Celeste. Rachel always had something to say – she had an opinion on everything. And he felt like he hadn't talked to her – *really* talked to her – in a long time.

'Do you want another drink?' Finn asked finally. He pushed a lock of hair off his forehead as he looked around the room. He wondered what Rachel was doing tonight. Knowing her, she was probably sitting at home, watching

A Star Is Born and drinking orange juice and ginger ale for her vocal cords.

'Uh, yes. Please.' Celeste smiled politely. She wasn't trying to be rude to poor Finn, but she was not enjoying her American party. 'Maybe just a glass of water?' American beer smelled like urine to her. At a French party, there would be bottles of nice wine, and the kids would not have to bribe a dirty older brother to buy it for them. Most French teenagers had been sampling wine at the dinner table for years, and it was not a big deal to have a glass or two among company.

In the family room, a cluster of people were playing Rock Band on a giant-screen TV. In the corner of the room, Puck and Rielle were sitting on a couple of leopard-print beanbags. Rielle, in a black T-shirt and a short black skirt, was sitting with her knees tucked to her side. 'They are terrible at that game,' she said, nodding toward the kids trying to finger the notes to 'Stairway to Heaven'.

Puck shifted closer so his knees were almost touching Rielle's. His pants were torn, so actually his bare knee was almost touching her knees, which unfortunately were covered in black tights. He would have liked a little more skin-to-skin contact. 'You should get up there. Show them how it's done.'

'I am not very good at classic rock.' Rielle smiled shyly at Puck. When she'd read those pages of notes with his words for lyrics neatly written out for her, she'd been completely surprised. She had underestimated Puck, clearly, as the lyrics were awesome – sensitive, smart, and funny. They even had some French words mixed in! Who knew what he was hiding underneath that funny haircut? What did the other kids keep calling it? A Mohawk?

I bet you're good at other things, Puck thought wickedly, staring at her lips. He was kind of having a hard time finding things to talk about with Rielle, and he wished they would hurry up and fast-forward to making out. 'Dude, what is that guy's deal?' Puck finally said, staring at the moody French guy with the gay ponytail. He was following ten feet behind Celeste and Finn as they walked into the kitchen, and he'd been lurking behind them all night like some kind of stalker.

Rielle looked up. 'Oh, Jean-Paul? He's just . . .'

Quinn was getting absolutely nowhere in her attempts to make both Puck and Finn unbearably jealous. Even when she'd strolled through the door, wearing a short black empire-waist dress and tiny braids at the sides of her loose hair, which hung in perfect waves over her bare shoulders, they didn't look up, even though her hand was clearly placed on Jean-Paul's arm.

Jean-Paul was, not surprisingly, a boring date. Even though he got her a bottled water when she asked him to, he couldn't seem to muster interest in anything she said and was always glancing around the room at other people. He kept kind of following Finn, too, which was fine with Quinn, as she was sure Finn would notice her at some point. But, really – what was wrong with her? She couldn't even attract a quiet, funny-smelling French guy with a biggish nose!

'Do you want to dance?' Quinn, bored out of her mind, asked Jean-Paul. Someone had switched the techno beat to better dance music, and people were pulling a glass-topped coffee table out of the way to clear a dance floor in the living room. She could see Celeste talking to Finn, and Rielle and Puck were walking toward the dance floor.

'Okay.' Jean-Paul shrugged, looking none too excited. He got to his feet slowly and ambled toward the dance floor. Everyone always watched to see who the first people to dance were. It was perfect timing for Quinn to make a move. After all, the spotlight always used to be on her. Now was her chance to regain a little of her former glory.

'You're a good dancer,' Quinn purred into Jean-Paul's ear after a few moments. It wasn't exactly true – he just kind of swayed back and forth – but boys liked to be complimented.

'Thanks,' he muttered, peering around the room.

Next to her, Santana, wearing a backless pink halter top from Mezzo and a pair of tight jeans, had grabbed the short, muscular French boy, and they were dancing furiously. Quinn had to hurry up and do something or everyone would be watching Santana instead.

Without thinking twice about it, Quinn grabbed Jean-Paul by the front of his shirt and pulled him in for a kiss. Immediately, the crowd exploded in a chorus of hollers and claps. Quinn knew that this was completely out of character for her, but she didn't care. Jean-Paul tasted like cigarettes and some weird kind of chewing gum.

But after only a few seconds of delicious attention, Jean-Paul broke away. He looked around the room desperately until his eyes locked with someone's – Celeste. An intense look passed between them before Celeste disappeared through the door to the kitchen. Even from the living room, with all the music and commotion, it was possible to hear the door to the backyard slam shut behind her.

'I'm sorry,' Jean-Paul said to Quinn. He backed away from her. 'I have to go.' Before she could say a word, he pushed past the other dancers. Quinn stepped back, trying to cover the awkwardness of the situation. The room suddenly felt overheated. Why was this happening to her?

Jean-Paul dashed around a brown velvet couch, crashing through the impromptu game of Twister that had sprung up, and hurried after Celeste. *What the heck is he doing?* thought Finn. *Why is* he *chasing after her, when* I'm *her date?* Feeling his knightlike instincts well up, Finn decided to follow them both and see what was going on. No one was going to mess with his girl.

Quinn, from the center of the room, quickly recovered

her shock. It was hard to pretend something hadn't happened when the entire room had seen it, but if anyone could do it, it was Quinn.

'What was that all about? You totally kissed that geeky French guy!' Santana said, coming up behind Quinn and putting a hand on her shoulder.

'It was so weird. We were just talking, and then he totally grabbed me and kissed me!' Quinn exclaimed, a scandalized look on her face. She pushed her hair out of her face. 'I don't know how they do things in France, but American girls are so not into PDA.'

Santana nodded wisely, although Quinn couldn't help thinking that *she* of all people, couldn't relate. Santana was frequently spotted locking lips with various football players in the halls of McKinley. 'What is going on now?' Santana said under her breath, looking over Quinn's shoulder.

Quinn turned around, thinking something else was happening with the messy little soap opera between Jean-Paul and Celeste, but this time, everyone was staring at the front door. During all the fuss, some party crashers had entered.

Party crashers of the worst kind. The Glee Club losers.

Mercedes led the pack through the room, and she was followed by her stinky French partner, Marc – or whatever his name was – Tina, Kurt, and a bunch of other French kids. They were all dressed up, and they actually looked kind of nice, even the dorky French guy. Santana's eyes narrowed. Was that shirt from Mezzo?

'Is that SingStar I see?' Kurt asked, already peering into the other room as if he had karaoke radar. A burly basketball player was butchering Maroon 5's latest single. Kurt rubbed his hands together deliciously. 'I don't think that boy has the proper angst to do that song justice.'

'Oh my God, we're going to rock this party. Do you think they have "Material Girl"?' Mercedes pulled Marc by the hand through the room toward the big-screen TV connected to the PlayStation. People stared at them, but they remained unflustered as they sank into an oversized couch to wait their turn. Not before long, however, Kurt and Aimee, who some guys thought looked very fetching in a low-cut red sweater dress, were belting out the 1980s hit 'Come on Eileen', and oversized basketball players with cups of warm beer were crowded around them, clapping.

'Do "Time After Time"!' Luke Wainwright called out when they finished. Others chimed in, shouting out their requests.

'It's like everywhere we go, those nerds are following us,' Quinn said, sinking defeatedly into the couch. She took a sip from a bottle of water. 'Where's Britt?'

'You won't believe it.' Santana pointed toward the family room, where Brittany was leaning over the shoulder of the French boy Marc. She was chewing on a piece of her long blond hair, which Santana and Quinn knew meant she was getting ready to pounce.

Outside, the night was clear and cold. Finn stood inside the back door for a moment, watching Celeste and Jean-Paul on the patio. They were talking – loudly – in French. Part of him thought maybe he shouldn't interrupt – but then Jean-Paul grabbed Celeste's arm. That was too much. Finn pushed open the door, the cold air hitting him with an icy blast. It felt kind of good after the sweatbox feel inside the house.

'What's going on here?' Finn demanded, rushing over the snow-covered patio to Jean-Paul. Jean-Paul was tall, but Finn had a good three inches and thirty pounds on him.

Jean-Paul let go of Celeste's arm. He looked exasperated. 'This is none of your business. Go away.' He tried to turn his back on Finn and get closer to Celeste, but Finn gave him a shove out of the way.

'Leave her alone,' Finn said, louder this time. He hated getting into fights, but if this guy wasn't going to stop harassing Celeste, he was going to get an American fist in his French face.

'You think you're such a tough basketball player, don't you?' Jean-Paul said. Inside, people crowded against the windows, hoping for a dramatic fight. 'Big American tough guy.' His breath was visible in a cloud. 'But you're really just a—'

'Stop!' Celeste shrieked, her soprano reaching an ear-splitting high. Finn and Jean-Paul immediately stepped away from each other. 'You boys are both crazy.' She looked freezing in her flimsy red tank top, and Finn wished he had a jacket to throw over her shoulders. She put her hand on Finn's arm, and he felt a surge of triumph. He'd won!

'You should go back inside. You're cold.' Finn tried to wrap an arm around Celeste, but she pushed him away. There was a full moon, and the backyard felt as light as day.

'Finn, Jean-Paul and I used to date, and he was just watching out for me.' She glanced at Jean-Paul and let go of Finn's arm. 'I got upset when I saw him kissing that blond cheerleader girl, okay?'

Finn took a step backward. The snow on the patio was a few inches deep, and it kept falling into the sides of his black Converse All Stars. He was going to have wet socks. He glanced at Jean-Paul, who was silent. 'Do you still . . . have feelings for him?'

Celeste rolled her eyes. 'It is not that easy. Just because a relationship ends does not mean your feelings completely shut off.' She rubbed her hands up and down her bare arms. 'He's also angry that I have decided to stay in America and attend school at McKinley.'

'What?' Finn almost tripped over a snow-covered patio chair. 'You're staying? That's so cool . . .' His mind was already reeling. He could really show Celeste America if she stayed. Take her out for ice cream or to the drive-in movie theater. There was still one that worked over in Royalton, and they always played the big summer blockbusters. He bet they didn't have that in France.

But . . . something else about what she said was hitting him, slowly. The thing about feelings.

'But listen to me.' Celeste looked Finn straight in the eyes. Her cheeks and lips had turned a bright red from the cold. 'There is nothing between us. You are a nice guy, but I was just . . . uh . . . trying you out.'

Finn blinked. *Trying me out?* Was that why she'd been acting kind of weird and distant all night? What the hell was wrong with these French girls? She was all over him in the locker room, and now, suddenly, that was just some kind of experiment? She could have just *said* something. These girls were just as crazy as the American ones!

Finn backed up, pointing at the two of them. 'You two . . . are both nuts. Really.' And he stormed back into the house, leaving them in the backyard to sort out their own feelings.

Meanwhile, Finn was thinking about his own.

Girls. They were all crazy. Like, for example, why the hell had Quinn been kissing Jean-Paul in the first place?

And weren't those some of the Glee kids who had shown up? Part of him wondered, just out of curiosity, if maybe Rachel was here. What Celeste had said was right, even if she was slightly off-kilter. Feelings don't just shut off. Finn's heart started to beat faster.

Maybe girls weren't the only unpredictable ones.

twenty-five

Multicultural Show, Saturday night

The McKinley High auditorium was filled to capacity on Saturday night. Students from several neighboring school districts participated in the show together every year, and the audience was packed with eager – and sometimes bored – parents. One extremely proud parent had brought her entire church group to watch her son perform 'We Are the World' on electric guitar.

There was no greenroom backstage, so many of the groups were preparing in the classrooms off the back hallway, while others were waiting in the hallway itself, repeatedly getting shushed by Jacob Ben Israel, otherwise known as 'J-Fro'. The geeky AV student always seemed to serve as stage manager for important shows, something he most likely volunteered to do as a way to gain more insider information for his blog.

'Your bra strap is showing, Rachel.' Jacob licked his lips and reached toward Rachel's white T-shirt, as if he was going to adjust it himself. 'It's quite alluring.'

Rachel jumped backward, knocking into a girl with a giant bassoonlike instrument. She adjusted her shirt. 'Jacob, I find it incredibly offensive that you use your position of stage manager as an excuse to sexually harass all the young female talent backstage.'

'I resent that implication. I was simply trying to help.' Jacob rubbed his hands together. He found Rachel's self-confidence – and pert bosom – intoxicating.

Those especially anxious to perform waited in the wings of the stage, silently watching the current performers from behind the heavy red velvet curtains, covered with a thin layer of dust, and worrying about their own acts. To a nervous high school student, the McKinley High auditorium could feel as big as Radio City Music Hall.

Before the show started, Principal Figgins, who had to give the welcome address, was going around the wings, talking briefly to each of the groups. 'Good luck,' he said, patting Mia Ng on the shoulder. She was a girl he saw only when she came to complain about her report-card grades every semester. The Asian Student Union members, carrying their brightly colored papier-mâché dragon costume, tried to keep the fluttery dragon wings from getting trampled on or tangled in the thick cords that opened and closed the velvet curtains. A group of Irish dancers, wearing outfits that made them look like leprechauns, did some last-minute practicing on their steps in the corner by the sound machine.

And taking up the most space were the Cheerios, all of them preparing for their performance about ethnic diversity. 'Oh my lord,' Principal Figgins muttered under his breath when he saw them.

They looked as if they were advertising the 'It's a Small World' exhibit at Disney World. Although they were in their Cheerios uniforms, the girls were carrying and waving flags and banners festooned with cartoonish illustrations of people from around the world. One flag featured an image of a Swiss Miss-type blonde with two braids in her hair, presumably representing Switzerland, while another banner showed an Asian girl in a snug-fitting silk Chinese dress holding hands with a tanned boy wearing a feathered headdress, a loincloth, and beaded moccasins. This was supposed to represent cultural unity? The Glee Club members collectively groaned when they noticed the flag that supposedly celebrated France: it featured a brunette wearing a French maid's outfit and carrying a feather duster.

'I don't think that's very PC,' Artie whispered to Kurt,

who was adjusting his hair in a prop mirror as the Glee Club members jockeyed for space backstage. 'The feather duster seems a little much.'

'Of course it's un-PC! It's Coach Sylvester!' It was hot backstage, and the warm air seemed to be negating the effectiveness of Kurt's carefully applied hairspray. 'I'm thinking about taking a picture of the Cheerios and sending it to the ACLU.'

The glee clubs had decided on a simpler route for their costumes. They all wore red pants or skirts with white T-shirts and navy blue cardigans, representing simultaneously the French and the American flags. The costumes were simple yet effective, and Kurt loved how he looked in red pants. He felt like he could stop traffic.

Principal Figgins eyed the Cheerios skeptically. It was useless to say anything now. Sue Sylvester knew how to put on a show, and she was armed with a fan base the size of a small Latin American country. 'Good luck, Sue,' he said tiredly as he passed.

'I stopped believing in things like Santa Claus and luck when I was two years old,' she snapped back. Coach Sylvester was wearing one of her tracksuits, a purple one with baby blue racing stripes down the sides. 'It's all about hard work, and my Cheerios worked on this routine until they were so exhausted, they could barely crawl off stage.'

'Hmm,' Principal Figgins replied. All it would take was

one parent who got fed up with Sue Sylvester's methods and the next thing he'd know, he'd have a class action lawsuit on his hands. 'Break a leg, then.'

He was about to move on to wish the next group good luck when he noticed Brittany dressed in her Cheerios uniform, waving a flag with an image of a Bollywood star, presumably to represent India.

'Sue, perhaps you didn't hear me yesterday when I told you that Santana and Brittany are not allowed to perform with the Cheerios. They've been caught leaving campus during school hours one too many times.'

'Figgins, you can't expect me to take *everything* you say seriously.' Coach Sylvester peered out at the audience. She loved to see a packed house. She could almost smell the anticipation in the air. Her Cheerios were going to blow all those cheesy mariachi bands and those untalented Glee kids out of the water.

'Sue, I am very serious about this. After the initial report of your girls' truancy from class, we did a little investigating. It turns out they've missed almost as many class periods as they've attended!' He turned to Santana and Brittany, who were staring humbly at the floor. 'You girls will come to my office first thing on Monday morning to discuss ways to make up the class time you've lost. And under no circumstances are you girls allowed to be part of the Cheerios performance.'

'Well, this is a disaster!' Coach Sylvester's face turned

purple with anger. 'Who's going to carry this flag?' Sue asked, pointing to the large silk flag that Santana had been halfheartedly waving over her head. It featured a woman wearing a full-body burka. 'I was making a very important comment on the subjugation of women.'

Principal Figgins sighed. Maybe this was working out for the best after all. 'I'm glad that's not going to happen. We have a few parents in the audience who would be offended by this performance.'

'We can't perform?' Brittany asked, as if she'd missed the entire conversation. Too much talking confused her. 'At all?' Brittany had promised her imaginary friend that she'd wave to him from the stage tonight.

'I am not a monster.' Principal Figgins adjusted his tie – black and decorated with Chinese characters he hoped didn't say anything offensive – and peeked out at a group of Central Valley High teenagers playing the African drums onstage. The floor beneath his feet was vibrating. 'As punishment, they can either not perform . . . or perform with Glee Club. It is up to you.'

'Glee Club? That is cruel and unusual punishment!' Sue Sylvester exclaimed. She eyed her girls for signs of insurgency. She had agreed to let them join Glee Club only in order to get inside information that might help her bring down Will Schuester for good, but she'd noticed over the last few months that – if she wasn't mistaken, which she never was – they were actually starting to enjoy it. It must be some sort of vocal hypnotherapy that witch doctor Will was practicing.

'I have a feeling the Glee kids, with a few notable exceptions, would be a better influence on these girls' attendance records than the rest of your Cheerios.' Most of the Glee kids were nerds, which meant that skipping class wouldn't even cross their minds. These Cheerios were too spoiled, too used to getting everything they wanted. And Principal Figgins was tired of getting medical notes from Coach Sylvester's dermatologist saying the girls needed to be excused early for mild glycolic facial peel sessions.

'Okay,' Brittany said quietly, stepping forward. She was afraid to look at Coach Sylvester, who'd be furious if the girls performed with Glee, but they had no choice. Besides, Mr Schuester had told them they could always come back, and that was something Coach Sylvester would never have said.

Besides, if she could still get onstage with Glee, her imaginary friend would be able to watch her do *something*. Brittany may have been a terrible student, but she was a totally amazing performer. Santana nudged her. 'Yes. Glee,' Brittany said absentmindedly.

'Ugh. *Fine*. I mean, I'll perform with Glee . . . if I have to.' Santana quickly seconded. She wasn't used to following Brittany's lead, but she was annoyed that Coach Sylvester wanted her to carry the worst flag as part of the Cheerios routine. A burka? That was so not sexy.

'I will not forget this, Figgins.' Coach Sylvester lowered her voice. She had so much blackmail evidence on Figgins – most of it manufactured – that she was honestly surprised that he was standing up to her on this. She was about to say something else, but he cut her off.

'I don't have time for this, Sue.' He pointed toward the stage. Students carrying drums of all sizes scurried off. 'And neither do you. You're on after the Irish dancers.'

Five minutes later, the two girls had shed their Cheerios uniforms and were dressed in the extra Glee outfits that Mr Schuester had brought along, just in case. He was always the optimist. Now that he had the rest of his members back, everything was really coming together. Even Quinn had shown up, looking a little burnt out but ready to go onstage. Mr Schuester patted Brittany on the back. 'I'm really glad you girls could join us. We need you.' As he said it, he gave Quinn a little wink to let her know he was speaking to her as well.

Quinn gave a measured smile, even though Mr Schuester's words were sweet to hear. It was nice to be needed. Even if Puck or Finn didn't need her, maybe Glee always would. She'd rather have a boy, but it wasn't a terrible backup plan.

'It all comes down to this,' Mr Schuester said in a stage whisper when the group had gathered around him. He didn't want to interrupt the Irish dancers, who were actually pretty good. Monsieur Renaud stood next to him, grinning from ear to ear. Brittany stepped closer to him and quietly tried to smell his Frenchness.

Mr Schuester continued, 'You've done an amazing job coming together over the past few days, and we are both really proud of each and every one of you. After the Cheerios number, we're on. I want you all to give it your best. Show the world what you're made of. Break a leg out there.'

Everyone had practiced the words to the songs until they were perfect, and even Mr Schuester's more linguistically challenged students were able to learn the French lyrics phonetically. '*And . . .*' Mr Schuester drew the word out. 'I've heard that Superintendent Doherty has taken his seat, front and center.'

'Hey, not to panic anyone or anything . . . but where's Celeste?' Finn scanned the backstage area. Even though he was still annoyed with her, it was strange that she wasn't back here with them, getting ready for the performance.

'What?' Mr Schuester's heart went cold. Celeste was an absolutely integral part of the show and had several solos. She couldn't be missing.

He immediately turned to Rachel, who, while he was doing his pep talk, was doing her annoying vocal warm-ups. Was it possible that she'd locked Celeste in a broom closet so that she could steal her parts? Had Mr Schuester made a huge mistake in letting her switch partners? Had this been her plan all along? 'Have you seen Celeste?'

But Rachel's voice sounded innocent as she quickly stopped her *br-br-br*-ing and replied, 'No, but I think I know where she is.'

'Hurry,' he advised, grabbing his hair with his fists. The audience broke into enthusiastic applause for the Irish dancers. Someone even threw roses on the stage. 'One more number, and then we're on.'

Rachel turned and ran down the hallways, her navy blue flats almost silent in the empty halls. She was hopeful that her hunch was right. Yesterday, she and Celeste had paused in the main atrium of the school to look at the giant trophy case that housed all the Glee Club awards from its successful run of years in the eighties and nineties. There were dozens of shiny gold trophies and plaques, engraved with the beautiful words MCKINLEY HIGH SCHOOL GLEE CLUB. Right smack in the middle was an oversized wood and gold trophy. Its engraved plaque read SECTIONAL CHAMPIONS 2010. Celeste had stared lovingly at the trophies, running her fingers along the glass and saying she wished her fellow glee club members took things more seriously.

On the stairwell opposite the trophy case, Celeste was sitting on the second step up, practicing some kind of measured yogalike breathing. Rachel's hunch was right.

'Celeste?' Rachel asked tentatively. She didn't want to interrupt the girl's meditation – she hated it when people interrupted her warm-up techniques – but Celeste looked more like she was freaking out than getting ready for the show. And they were on next. 'Are you okay?'

Celeste looked up. Her blue eyes were watery. 'I don't think I can go back there. I don't think I can see Jean-Paul again. You see, he is the old boyfriend who cheated on me and broke my heart.' She rubbed her temples with her fingers. Her nails were long and red, and Rachel wished she'd thought to paint her nails red for the show tonight. 'And now he wants me back!'

'Oh.' Having had very limited romantic experience herself – several flings at performing arts summer camps and her all-too-brief relationship with Finn – Rachel didn't consider herself very capable of giving romantic advice. She glanced down the hallway to the doors of the auditorium, wishing someone else were there to give Celeste a boy-drama pep talk.

But the auditorium was full of people waiting to be wowed by the Glee Club performance, and Rachel owed it to her teammates to talk Celeste down from her tree and get her onstage. 'Who cares what *he* wants? You need to do what *you* want. You're far more important than he is, and not just because you're talented.' Rachel smiled. 'You're a nice person.'

Celeste shrugged. She looked miserable. 'The real reason I wanted to come to America to go to school in the first place was not only the career opportunities – although that was a factor – but mostly to get away from Jean-Paul.'

'You want to . . . go to school here? At McKinley?' Rachel felt a shiver down her spine. That was what she was doing in Miss Pillsbury's office? Trying to transfer? Rachel had just come to terms with Celeste's talent and had finally started to really like her – but that would all change if she suddenly became a permanent member of Glee Club.

Celeste shook her head slowly. 'I don't know anymore.' A tear slid down her cheek.

Rachel wasn't sure what to do, but she hated to see anyone this unhappy. Her next words weren't motivated entirely by self-interest. Rather, she felt a real connection to Celeste, and she thought she understood where she was coming from. 'Celeste, don't you see? You shouldn't let him push you around like that, especially after how he treated you! You're letting a *boy* determine your destiny!'

'I am?' Celeste looked up at Rachel.

Rachel sat down next to her, feeling a rush of empathy for her French partner. Just because she was gorgeous didn't mean she had better luck with boys than Rachel did, although she did have a perfect nose. 'Going to America to avoid a boy would be the same thing as going to America *for* a boy. Don't worry about Jean-Paul. He clearly needs to be medicated, and he's not worth getting upset over.'

'I don't know.' Celeste sighed softly and stared up at

238

the artwork lining the walls of the stairwell. Pretty ink drawings of Japanese characters hung, slightly crooked, above them. 'It *would* be good for my career, though.'

'Coming to Lima?' Rachel asked incredulously. In the back of her mind, she knew that, as much as she liked Celeste, she simply could not deal with her at McKinley. It would be an absolute disaster. *Rachel* might have to transfer. 'Lima is not exactly the most cosmopolitan of cities, and just because it's closer to Broadway than France it doesn't mean there are more opportunities.'

Rachel could see that Celeste was starting to perk up – maybe she wasn't so excited about the idea of transferring to McKinley anyway. 'Besides, someone like you will have an amazing career *wherever* you are. Your talent will help you find your way.' Surprisingly, Rachel was being sincere. She grabbed Celeste's hand and squeezed it.

Celeste smiled her million-watt smile. A dimple in her cheek appeared, which Rachel wished *she* had – it would look so great in head shots. 'You think so?' she asked Rachel, although it was clear she already agreed with her.

'Definitely. And your glee club needs you.' Rachel tucked a loose lock of hair behind her ear, careful not to snag it on her favorite gold star stud earrings. 'I mean, imagine where the McKinley Glee Club would be without me.' She shivered. She liked to think about that every once in a while, just to remind herself how important she was. 'That's where yours would be without you.'

'That is true. They are all quite talented, but no one has perfect pitch like I do.' Celeste was already staring into the distance. Rachel recognized that look – she was imagining herself onstage, the rapt audience waiting for her to open her mouth and amaze them. Rachel didn't want to spoil the moment by telling her she didn't exactly have perfect pitch – she was a tiny bit sharp. But only someone with an ear as finely tuned as Rachel's was would notice.

'Do you think you're ready to go up onstage and show everybody what we've got?' Rachel asked a little anxiously. She got to her feet and smoothed out her red skirt. Mr Schuester had probably bitten off his nails with worry by now. She was glad the pep talk was working and all, but she didn't want to be late.

But Celeste quickly jumped up, also eager to get back. She started tugging Rachel toward the auditorium. 'Yes, let's go. You are right about everything. I belong at home, for now. And it doesn't matter where Jean-Paul is – he is not for me.'

A wave of relief washed over Rachel. She liked Celeste and all, but McKinley High didn't exactly have room for two stars, and Rachel wasn't about to give up her spot to anyone.

'Just in time!' Mr Schuester exclaimed when he saw Celeste and Rachel appear backstage. Tiny beads of sweat had formed along his hairline. 'I was just starting to freak out.' He didn't want to say it, but he'd actually been enjoying the Cheerios performance – because it was terrible. Without Sue's best girls, the routine was completely thrown off, and the song – as well as the over-the-top banners – came off as tacky and distasteful. Mr Schuester didn't normally feel good about taking pleasure in other people's misfortune, but Sue Sylvester could deal with a good dose of humility. 'Are you all ready?'

This time, everyone responded. As soon as Sue's lack-luster Cheerios stumbled backstage, the Glee kids headed out. Maybe it was the advantage of having the slot right after a terrible performance, but the second the kids burst into their poppy mash-up of 'Love Train' and 'L'Hymne à L'Amour', the audience was one hundred percent behind them. From his spot behind the curtain, Mr Schuester could see Mr Doherty in the front row tapping his feet to the beat and whispering to his wife, who was wearing a short skirt and looked twenty years younger than he was.

But even though the budget money would be nice, he thought, it couldn't compare to the sight of these two distant glee clubs coming together so successfully. That was priceless.

twenty-six

McKinley High parking lot, Sunday morning

fter the Multicultural Show on Saturday night, Monsieur Renaud and Mr Schuester decided to reward the two teams on their successful performance by taking them out to the Lima Freeze. Even though it wasn't exactly ice-cream season, no one objected, not even the Cheerios, who ordered frozen yogurt. (After all, they didn't burn as many calories singing as they would have dancing with the rest of the cheerleading squad.) The large group had stayed at the ice-cream shop until closing, the kids leaning over booths talking to one another in French and English as they slurped down their milk shakes and sundaes.

That didn't mean the Glee kids were ready to say

good-bye to their French counterparts yet. Even before Mr Schuester could suggest it, Rachel asked him, shyly, if it would be possible to see the French kids off in the morning before their bus took them to the Columbus airport.

And so, on Sunday morning, not too early, the McKinley High Glee Club straggled into the parking lot at school. It was one of those late winter days where the sun was shining so brightly the snow was almost blinding, and, although it was cold, the blueness of the sky made everyone think of spring. Tina had gone over to Kurt's house early in the morning to make a banner, as Kurt always seemed to have a healthy stash of crafting supplies. They had made a long white banner saying AU REVOIR, LES AMIS in glittery gold paint – they got the phrase by Googling *French translation for 'good-bye, friends'*.

The Glee kids were all holding up the banner – even Quinn, Santana, and Brittany had shown up – when the French kids' bus pulled up and they tumbled out into the cold.

Celeste was the first person off the bus. She gave Rachel a fierce hug and slipped a piece of paper with her address into Rachel's hands. 'Send me a playbill when you make it to Broadway.' Then she went to each McKinley student and gave them kisses on their cheeks, saying, 'Thank you for all your support.'

After she kissed Kurt, he whispered to Mercedes, 'I'm seriously not going to miss Rachel's French twin. I fully appreciate that she has hair that looks like it belongs in a Pantene commercial, but having two Rachels around makes my head want to explode.'

'Did you hear good news from your superintendent yet?' Monsieur Renaud asked as he and Mr Schuester hugged and patted each other on the back. The Cheerios were waving flirtatiously at the French teacher, and he tried to politely ignore them.

'Uh . . . no.' Mr Schuester frowned sheepishly. 'And I'm afraid I'm not going to. He called me last night to tell me that he was incredibly impressed with our kids' performance. But . . . the board decided that the money won't be going to any activities after all. Due to recent record-breaking reports of food poisoning, they've decided to funnel the extra money into a new refrigeration system for the cafeteria instead.'

'Oh, no!' Monsieur Renaud exclaimed. 'That is terrible. Although I did eat a bite of that *palak paneer* and thought I might pass out.'

'I know. Apparently, you weren't the only one. The refrigerators weren't working properly all week.' Mr Schuester eyed his kids, who were all kissing cheeks and laughing. He wished he'd thought to bring his video camera. At least the AV club had videotaped last night's performance for him from the audience. He'd show it to the kids on Monday. 'I guess if we want to make it to France, we'll have to do it the hard way.'

'Bake sales and car washes?' Monsieur Renaud suggested.

Mr Schuester grinned. 'Sounds like it!' It wasn't the worst news in the world. At the very least, the Cheerios performance had been absolutely horrendous, and they weren't going to receive a dime of the money, either. That was satisfaction enough. And at least no one would get sick after lunch now.

More satisfying, though, was the sight of the students exchanging addresses and e-mails. Angelique had, very quietly, invited Tina to visit her in Lyon and check out the art museums. Even though she was just as shy as Tina, they'd apparently made a real connection. Gerard, even though he hadn't exactly hit it off with Puck, had made friends with other jocks, and he was wearing a slightly too large McKinley football jacket that he'd won in a pull-up contest against one of them. Mercedes and Marc were already planning on collaborating on more songs online, and, surprisingly, it looked as if Puck and Rielle were having a tender good-bye.

Artie looked on from the sidewalk. Because it was Sunday, the sidewalk hadn't been shoveled, and it was hard to get his wheelchair to move through the slush. His gloved hands were wet from turning the snow-covered wheels. It seemed like he was doomed to sit on the sidelines, watching the good-looking but morally reprehensible guy get the girl. He still hadn't said anything to Rielle about Puck stealing his lyrics, because it seemed kind of petty and childish, and besides, he'd resigned himself to his fate. He'd look silly saying something now, anyway, although he did feel kind of bad letting Rielle think there was more to Puck than meets the eye, when, in fact, there was less.

'I hope you will send me more of your amazing lyrics,' he heard Rielle say to Puck. Artie stared at the bare trees in the distance, feeling the exact same way he had felt after eating the cafeteria food on Mexican day, only worse.

'Of course, babe.' Artie couldn't look up, but he imagined Puck was leaning in to kiss Rielle.

Then Rielle came over to talk to Artie. She had on a short leather jacket over a long red sweater, and a red knit cap was pulled down over her short hair. 'Artie.' She smiled. 'It was lovely to meet you.'

Artie's fingertips suddenly felt warm. 'Hey, Rielle. Have a safe trip back to France.' *Really?* he thought as soon as the words came out of his mouth. That was the best he could come up with? Maybe she was better off with Puck.

Before he knew what she was doing, Rielle leaned forward. Her mouth was distractingly close to his ear. *'Les yeux marron, les lèvres rouges fait le coeur bleu.'*

Artie's jaw dropped. It was one of the lyrics he'd written for her.

'*Merci beaucoup* for the wonderful lyrics, Artie.' She

smiled down at him warmly. 'I am going to work them all into my songs. You are a real poet.'

'You *knew*?' Suddenly, his whole body felt warm. It didn't matter if he never saw Rielle again, as long as she knew those words came from him, and not from the stunted brain of Puck. 'How did you figure it out?'

Rielle's brown eyes widened. 'At the party on Friday. I was talking to Puck, and I realized he was . . . uh . . . how do you say it?' She thought for a minute. 'A total idiot.'

Artie almost choked on his laughter.

Rielle continued, stomping her feet to keep warm. 'I tried to mention the French things in the songs, and he . . . had no idea what I was saying.' She shook her head. 'He does not speak any French.'

'That makes sense,' Artie admitted. He felt like he was flying. 'Puck hasn't mastered his native language yet, much less any foreign ones.' Rielle leaned forward again, her breath tickling Artie's nose as she gave him a soft kiss on the cheek. His whole face burned. 'So why did you ask him to send you more lyrics?'

Rielle giggled and pulled away. 'I just wanted to see the look on his face.' She handed him a folded piece of paper with her address, her e-mail, and even her phone number on it. 'It is really you who I hope will send me more lyrics.'

'You'll have to send me recordings of your songs, then.'

Artie couldn't believe it. He was actually going to have a hot French pen pal. Maybe it wasn't as good as a hot French girlfriend, but he had to start somewhere.

'Yes.' Rielle glanced toward the bus, which was starting to fill up with French students. '*Au revoir*,' she whispered before she turned and walked away. Artie's heart felt like it was about to burst.

On the other side of the crowd, Finn was standing by himself, hands stuffed into his pockets, when Celeste, looking gorgeous in a thick white scarf and matching cap, ran up to him. Her cheeks were flushed pink from the cold, and her long blond hair tumbled out from beneath her hat. 'Finn!' she exclaimed. She had a slightly sheepish smile on her face. 'I want to apologize to you. It was very rude of me to use you like that, and I am very sorry.'

Finn stared at the ground. Celeste *had* used him, and tossed him out like a piece of trash when she was done with him. Making out with him and then moving on seemed like such a . . . well, such a *guy* thing to do. He wanted to stay mad at her . . . but she was just too pretty. How could anyone stay mad at a hot girl?

He glanced up at her, and as soon as he did, it was all over. She looked like she should be skiing down the slopes in the Alps – those were in France, right? 'It's okay,' he found himself saying. 'It's not a big deal.'

Celeste touched his arm. Even though she had mittens

on, and he had on his heavy winter coat, he felt like his arm was burning. 'You are such a sweetheart.'

He shrugged modestly. Although no guy loved being called a 'sweetheart', anything from Celeste sounded sexy. 'You know . . . you can always call me, if you ever, you know, change your mind.'

A tiny smile played on Celeste's lips. 'Yes, if that ever happens.' She waved a white mitten at Finn and turned toward the bus. The rest of the students were boarding, although there was a cluster of girls waiting at the open bus door, reluctant to leave. They were Aimee, Sophie, and Claire – Kurt's fan club.

Aimee broke away from the others and rushed toward Kurt, giving him one last hug. The other two girls jealously followed, and all three almost swallowed Kurt in a bear hug.

'Good-bye, ladies.' Kurt disentangled himself from the girls and smoothed out the front of his Marc Jacobs peacoat. 'I will miss you all.'

As they sadly boarded the bus, they all blew kisses at Kurt and waved frantically. 'Good-bye, Kurt. Write to me!' Claire called.

'Write to me!' Aimee called, a little louder. She was the last one on the bus, and the folding door almost closed on her. From the fogged-up windows, the French kids fondly waved good-bye. Slowly, the bus pulled away from the curb.

Meanwhile, the rest of Glee Club turned to Kurt. 'How did you get three chicks?' Puck asked jealously. He looked Kurt up and down. He wasn't even buff like Puck was. 'Don't they know you're . . . you know . . . into dudes?'

Kurt straightened his shoulders. 'They confused gay and European – such a common mistake.' He adjusted the beret that he'd worn for the occasion. 'Who was I to correct them? Besides, they agreed to send me the newest French fashions before they come out in the States.'

'Playah!' Puck called out, holding his hand up for a high five. Everyone laughed as Kurt slapped it.

Mr Schuester clapped his hands together. 'How about as a celebration of a job well done, you let me take you all out for lunch?'

The Glee Club members hooted and stomped their feet.

'What do you say?' he asked, grinning from ear to ear. 'French fries, anyone?'

CALLING ALL gleeks!

There are three official Glee novels that no self-respecting Gleek will want to be without.

GLEE: THE BEGINNING
£6.99
Available now
978 0 7553 7737 4

Get more of your favourite characters in this official Glee prequel! All great performances deserve a warm-up! Enroll early at McKinley High to find out what went on before New Directions was even a glimmer in Mr Schuester's eye. When did Rachel first decide Finn was more than just a jock? When did Puck and Quinn start their secret romance? And how did the fledgling Glee Club function without a fearless leader? Hint: It wasn't exactly a perfect melody. Break out the gold stars and refill the frozen drinks: it's time to find out what happened to all your favourite characters *before* the show-mance began.

GLEE: FOREIGN EXCHANGE
£6.99
Available in February
978 0 7553 7738 1

Can Rachel Berry rock a beret? McKinley High goes international when a French glee club comes to town in the second original Glee novel. Kurt gets an entourage, Finn falls for a new girl, and Puck learns that some moves are lost in translation in this hilarious culture-clash story.

GLEE: SUMMER BREAK
£6.99
Available in July
978 0 7553 7739 8

Mr Schuester doesn't want the Glee Club to lose its momentum over summer break, so he's talked Rachel, Finn and the crew into running a singing workshop for local kids.